I0620862

FAIRYTALE FOUND

A Queen's City Novel

Lori A. Hendricks

Illipsium Publishing
Virginia Beach, Virginia

Lori A. Hendricks/Illipsium Publishing
P.O. Box 61383
Virginia Beach, VA 23466
www.loriahendricks.com

Publisher's Note: This is a work of fiction. Names, characters, places, and incidents are a product of the author's imagination. Locales and public names are sometimes used for atmospheric purposes. Any resemblance to actual people, living or dead, or to businesses, companies, events, institutions, or locales is completely coincidental.

Book Layout ©2013 BookDesignTemplates.com

Ordering Information:
Quantity sales. Special discounts are available on quantity purchases by corporations, associations, and others. For details, contact the "Special Sales Department" at the address above.

Fairytale Found/ Lori A. Hendricks. -- 1st ed.
ISBN 978-0-9964403-7-0

Dedicated to the hopeless romantic in all of us.

Forever is composed of nows.

–EMLY DICKINSON

J axson was pissed. Like, good and righteously furious. *Some vacation*, he thought angrily as he crawled on his belly through a busted basement window. He paused at the sound of the fabric of his blast suit snagging the jagged glass. He'd been happily on his way to visit his brother and niece for some much-needed time away from the base. The cross-country drive was soothing to the bitterness that grew within him. He wasn't exactly sure the cause of the anger, but he knew if he couldn't control it, it would mean the end of his career in the Corps.

When his work mobile rang, he gave serious thought to not answering, but with Jaxson duty always won. And now he was helping state and local authorities in downtown Charlotte, North Carolina find a bomb in the lobby of an office tower downtown. He was officially a dumbass.

"Jax? Jax, man, come in." A voice buzzed loudly in his earpiece belonging to Sullivan. He'd been Jaxson's classmate at the academy and was currently his partner in this insane endeavor. Jaxson grimaced at the intrusion, though he was relieved at being pulled away from his darkening thoughts.

"Jesus Christ Sully take the damn mic out of your fucking mouth," he whispered harshly. He and Sullivan had been assigned to the same explosive ordinance unit for the US Marine Corps for the past three years after graduating together from the US Naval Academy. And coincidentally, both men had grown up in the Charlotte metropolitan area. It made sense to work together on this, even if Jaxson's ear drums couldn't survive his partner's excited tone. Sullivan's "devil may care" attitude drove Jax crazy and there'd been more times than he could count that he'd wanted to throw Sullivan onto a bomb rather than help him disarm it, but there was no one who was better at his job.

Sullivan chuckled. "Jax, the bombers are still in the building. I am going to try entering through the service entrance in back. We'll rendezvous in the lobby."

"Roger that. And for once, please, try to be quiet. We don't need the damn building coming down on our heads." Jaxson rolled his eyes at the sound of Sullivan's snicker. He wondered for at least the hundredth time how they ended up here when this was clearly in the jurisdiction of the FBI or ATF.

Shaking those thoughts out of his head he focused on the room around him, his attention quickly zooming in on the electrical panel that dominated the far wall. Three snips and power for the lobby and elevators was cut. He slowly made his way to the stairwell on the other side of the room, his service weapon drawn, cocked and ready. He was halfway up to the main level when gunshots rang out over his head.

"Goddamn it, Sully," he growled before breaking into a sprint across the basement to the doorway and staircase, taking the stairs two at a time. Jaxson paused at the door to the lobby and listened. The gunshots were moving away from his location toward the back of the building - right where Sullivan was supposed to be. As always, Sully's impetuous nature had gotten his crazy ass in trouble, except this time, Jaxson wasn't sure he'd be able to save his friend from himself.

Slowly and as quietly as possible, he turned the handle of the heavy metal door. There were bodies littering the lobby's marble floor, including one man wearing what appeared to be a suicide bomber vest. Understanding flowed over and through him as his mind grasped exactly what they were dealing with, and why they'd been called in to handle the situation. Suicide bombers with dead hostages. This was bad. Jaxson needed to get to Sullivan. He slipped through the door unseen, crouching low, hiding behind a column, and letting the door close loudly. Hoping to draw some of the fire away from his friend, he aimed true and shot one of the bombers in the neck. He couldn't see Sullivan from his vantage point, but soon he heard the familiar buzzing in his ear.

"You gotta get out," Sullivan groaned. "I'm hit and the asshole in charge of this shit show has started the timer for the big bomb to blow. All the hostages are dead. You've got less than thirty seconds, man. Run." Another groan followed by a slow wet exhale. "Run!"

Jaxson hesitated and wondered briefly if he could save Sullivan.

"Sullivan." he whispered angrily, then waited for a response. Getting none, he looked around the column, spotting the nearest exit. Ten feet and two bombers who were either planning to die in the blast or hadn't been told the countdown was on lay between him and escape. He took off running, firing his gun as he went. One bomber went down quickly, but the other fired back, hitting Jaxson in the leg. Ignoring the burning pain that radiated across his calf, he turned and fired his gun. Refusing to slow down, he shot the lobby's main glass doors, shattering it. The building blew as he jumped through the door, the force of the blast blowing him clear of the building but giving him severe burns on his back and legs despite the protection of his blast suit. As he landed on the concrete, his mind went to Sullivan and he said a quick prayer for his best friend and old partner. The intense pain pulled him under, then his mind went black.

2

The first time Jaxson woke up from his medically induced coma he cracked his eyes open to find his older brother, father, and two-year-old niece in his room. He'd been dreaming of Sullivan and the beach in San Diego. They had been reminiscing about their last deployment and homecoming. Sully's most recent fling met them at the boat with a big wet kiss and tight hugs. Sully always did have the best taste in women even if he didn't behave any better than a horny teenager in behavior.

Jaxson didn't like thinking about his lost comrade in arms. His pain had been dulled by the medication, but his mind held on to the memory of the sounds and smells of the office building coming down around him. It was a pain he hadn't had to feel in quite a while – his unit had been beyond lucky as to not have suffered a direct loss in more than five deployments. So, he swallowed his tears and forced his eyes to open fully.

He took stock of his situation. There was a tube in his mouth and down his throat. His lips were taped shut and there was an oxygen tube in his nostrils. Jaxson tried to move his arms and found that one was in a hard wrap – likely a cast and tethered to the bed. He didn't have the strength to move his legs, but he could wiggle his toes and decided that was good enough.

Jaxson's eyes swung around the room, taking in his surroundings. His generally stoic father was in tears, and little Ava was telling her grandpa that Uncle Jax had two eyes, and to be happy. Jaxson blinked hearing his niece's heavy voice. She was going to sound just like her mother, he dreamily thought. The tracheotomy tube in his mouth and throat made it impossible for him to speak. Before too long a bunch of nurses and doctors descended on him, poking, and prodding his still very tender skin. His pain fueled moans instantly upset the little girl, causing his brother and father to take her out of the room. By the time they had returned, the medical staff had finished torturing him and were on their way out, and Jaxson was beginning to relax as the pain medication hit his blood stream.

His father, an old-school gruff manly man, leaned down and kissed Jaxson's forehead, tears gathering in his eyes yet again. Jaxson and his father rarely saw eye to eye. They were entirely too much alike to have ever really gotten along. But at no time in his life did Jaxson ever question his father's love and devotion, and now, Jaxson felt tears well up in his own eyes. The old man may make him crazy, but Jaxson would move heaven and hell for the old grump. His brother, Lukas, placed a soft but callused hand on Jaxson's cheek - one of the few unburned patches of skin left on his body. And then his brother held little Ava down for a soft kiss. They left as Jaxson fell into a comfortable, restful sleep.

The second time he woke up he had absolutely no idea what time of day it was. His curtained off space in the Intensive Care Unit didn't have windows or a clock. The room was dark and all he could hear was the beeping of the machines. His arms and chest were so heavily bandaged, that he doubted he wore a watch, and in any case, he still couldn't move his arms to check.

Jaxson mentally tried to shake off the remaining cobwebs of a dream. He was trapped in rubble trying to find his partner. Unable to move to free himself or Sully, he cried out in frustration – or so it seemed. In reality, he was only able to choke himself on the tube in his mouth. Once he got his breathing regulated, his eyes adjusted to the darkness and he looked around the room.

"It's eight p.m. on October the tenth," came a vaguely familiar voice from somewhere near the foot of the bed.

Jaxson tried to lift his head to see who was there, but the tubes in his nose and mouth restricted nearly all movement in his upper body. Jaxson struggled to place the voice, but his brain was so addled by the medication any coherent thought slipped away before he could grab ahold of it. The person, a woman - he was fairly certain - took pity on him and arose from her seat. She moved slowly, making her way to Jaxson's bedside. She reached over and flipped on the small spotlight, so Jaxson could see her clearly without straining his eyes.

Her scent. His brain couldn't believe what his eyes saw, but the faint scent of amber musk and vanilla always gave her away.

Lee watched him sadly as first understanding and then recognition flittered across Jaxson's bruised and battered face. She gave him a small smile and a low "Hello" as his eyes lit up, staring unblinkingly at her.

Unable to resist, she leaned down and placed a soft kiss on his dry cheek. She sighed deeply as the familiar burn in her gut churned. She tried to pull herself away, but Jaxson's good arm twined around her neck and urged her forward into a deeper hug. Using a hand braced on the bed, Lee pushed herself up, out of his grasp. It took a few seconds longer to pull herself together.

"Your father and brother recognized me while I was talking to security about visiting you. Your brother was kind enough to approve my visitation today, much to your dad's dismay." Lee grimaced at the memory of Jax's father's disapproving frown. Luckily Lukas saved her from embarrassing herself in the hospital. She had been prepared to beg if necessary.

Lee had been sitting by the foot of his bed for the last thirty minutes trying to figure out what to say to this man, who'd broken her heart and then haunted her dreams for the last four years. As he slept, she'd replayed their last conversation in her mind a dozen times, trying to decide what she should and should not tell him. There was so much she wanted to say, needed to say and still so much she wasn't sure she could say. Judging from what she could see and what she'd overheard the doctors say, Jaxson was in for several months of surgeries and some intensive rehabilitation. Could she, in good consciousness, add to that burden in any way?

His eyes were pinned to her face - part anger, part confusion. Jaxson struggled against the tubes briefly before relaxing against the pillow in defeat.

"I'll go if my being here bothers you," Lee said sadly. She never intended to hurt him with this visit. But after seeing him on the news being wheeled out of the blast rubble on a gurney, she needed to see with her own eyes that he was still alive.

Every time she'd heard he was in town she consciously stayed away from any spot he'd likely be, despite the fact that she still missed him almost painfully. Jaxson was a creature of habit and she had known him well enough that it was relatively easy to avoid an unwanted confrontation. She effectively put off any difficult conversation they needed to have. She'd been living a kind of double life with their mutual friends. Lee had been careful to never betray her secrets, yet never giving anyone a reason to mention her to him - like they seemed to always do to her when he visited his family in the city. She knew all about his exploits and battles. Sometimes it was too much. Most times really.

But now he was lying here in front of her and she needed to finally come clean. Time was short, and her day of reckoning may have finally come.

Her biggest secrets where his as well and though she wanted to keep hiding, it was time Jaxson knew the truth. Lee hoped he could handle it.

He stared at her before abruptly shaking his head no. Lee released the breath she'd held unconsciously. A dismissal now would make what needed to happen so much more difficult. She finally had gotten the nerve to confront him - any further delay would likely kill her resolve.

"I - I just wanted to see for myself that you were going to be okay," she said softly. "Can I get you anything?"

Jaxson mimed writing with his left hand; one bit of luck Jaxson was a natural lefty since the right hand was in a hard plaster cast up to his elbow.

Lee nodded and walked out to the nurse's station, requesting a pen and pad. After promising to bring Jaxson a small whiteboard and markers for use in the future, the nurse reluctantly handed over the requested items. When Lee returned, Jaxson's eyes were shut, and his breathing was even. She hesitated before deciding to leave the pad and pen on the table closest to Jaxson's left hand. She gently stoked her hand over his bruised but unburned cheek. She turned to leave, and his hand grabbed hers, and he held on tightly. She lowered her eyes to his and it took all her willpower to hold his gaze and not run out the door or worse. She leaned down and softly kissed him again.

Jaxson tried to yawn but with the tape on his mouth it was more of a grunt and whine. He released Lee's hand to hold his breathing tube steady. She took a step back and though he tried to pretend he didn't notice, her guilty expression said that he'd failed.

"I'll let you get some rest," she whispered, rubbing the spot of her wrist that he'd held. "I really should go." Lee grabbed her bag out of the chair and turned to go. A light metallic tapping caught her attention. She turned back to Jaxson and saw he was struggling to write and hold the pad steady with just his left hand. Lee walks back to Jaxson's bedside and peered down at the chicken scratch on the paper.

"Return," she read off the page and Jaxson nodded his head in agreement. "Sure," she replied.

He held up a finger for her to wait and scribbled another word on the pad.

"Tomorrow," it had said, but Lee shook her head. "I can't come tomorrow. But I can come on Friday," she said, instantly regretting putting a solid date on her return. Lee leaned down and patted Jaxson's hand, bidding him a quiet good night before slipping between the curtains and leaving Jaxson to his quiet thoughts.

FAIRYTALE FOUND

3

Jaxson watched helplessly as Lee more or less ran from his bedside. He was certain she was a figment of his drug addled imagination. But the feeling of her lips on his face was very real – as was his body's reaction. She was still the most gorgeous woman that he'd ever laid eyes on. And that walk - it hadn't changed in all this time. Her sexy sashay was one of the first things to attract him to her. His eyes had been glued to her perfect backside when she left, and the rest of his body responded to that seductive little wiggle in her walk.

He didn't want her to leave. Her voice was soothing and while she was around, he'd swear the pain seemed to drift further away. *Why she had really come*, he wondered. She'd said something about wanting to know that he was really okay, but was that all there was to it? He didn't know, and he wouldn't know for sure until she came back. If she came back, that is. Now that he knew she was still in Charlotte, he'd find her. He'd convinced himself that she'd moved back to Kenya with her mother and sister. It was how he'd convinced himself that she wasn't waiting for him still. But that wasn't the case. And now he wouldn't accept anything less than giving her a full explanation for why he'd left her fall those years ago. But first, he had to get rid of this damned breathing tube.

Lee made it to the sliding metal door of the ICU ward before tearing up. By the time she made it to her car she was in a full blubber. It took her five minutes to pull herself together enough to drive home safely. And yet another five to trust her voice enough to speak. Sitting at a red light, she pulled the business card Lukas had given her from her shirt pocket and dialed the number. Luckily her phone was integrated into the car's stereo system so Lee could focus on holding in her tears instead of holding the phone.

Lukas answered on the second ring. His voice was the same as it had always been – clear and strong. But Lee could sense there was a tinge of sadness in his tone that hadn't been there when she first met him. Lee wondered what had caused it.

Lee hesitated before responding. "Hi," she got out. Barely.

She wasn't sure Lukas had heard her, but he replied, "Lee. Hi. How is Jaxson?"

Straight to the point and so unlike the happy go lucky Lukas she'd known before. She wondered again what had happened that could change him so fundamentally.

"He was on his way to sleep when I left. He asked me for a pen and paper, so he could communicate. I got it from the nurses' station, but I had to promise the nurse on duty that someone would bring him a small whiteboard and markers."

"Oh good," Lukas exclaimed. "He hadn't been communicative before now." Lukas paused, then pushed forward. He needed answers and the only person he could get them from was the skittish woman on the other end of this phone call.

"Lee," he started carefully. "Why did you visit my brother today? As far as I know, you two haven't spoken in years."

Lee took a deep breath, then released it slowly. She knew this was coming but it didn't make her answer any easier. "I simply needed to see for myself that he was okay. If he'd sent me away, I would have left and never come back," she added quickly.

Lukas took his time and absorbed her words sure they were only part of the story. "And then," he asked, laying the real question out there.

"He asked me to come back and I agreed. Lukas, I have no ulterior motive." A lie of omission, but she pushed on. "I saw the explosion and I know how Jaxson is. I was worried. That's all."

Lee stopped talking before she said too much. She could only hope Lukas could accept her at her word.

"I see" was all he said. He gave her a quick goodbye and hung up.

Lee couldn't relax. She hated lying and she knew that once the truth came out, Lukas would be furious with her. But she also knew the right answer was for her to tell Jaxson the truth herself, and not anyone else. Lee was running out of time all right. She sighed heavily and continued home.

Lukas could tell that Lee was hiding something, but she'd given no indication about what that something could be. He'd briefly considered pressuring her for additional answers and quickly dismissed that idea. Whatever she was hiding was most likely between her and Jaxson. It really wasn't any of his business. Lukas knew how much leaving her had hurt his brother, but Jaxson's decisions - no matter how asinine - were his own. Jaxson had put his military career ahead of all of his relationships and when he left on his first deployment, he could not or would not tell Lee what was happening. Lukas couldn't blame Lee for what went down, but his natural instinct was to protect his daft little brother if at all possible. He didn't know exactly what was coming, but it was clear there was still unfinished business between his brother and the only woman that had been able to capture his heart.

4

Lukas dropped Ava at the babysitter's house before heading to the hospital. She adored her uncle Jax, but also repeated everything she heard, and Lukas didn't want his father to have any more reasons to dislike Lee. That stubborn old man held on to grudges like gorilla glue – even when he was wrong.

He remembered to pick up the whiteboard and markers and carried them with him as he entered the ICU wing. The nurse on duty gave him a thumbs up when he lifted the items for inspection.

They had been explicit when detailing what Jaxson was and was not allowed to have while in ICU.

Jaxson was propped up in bed when he arrived. The breathing tube had been disconnected from the larger machine.

"Hey little brother," Lukas said as a way of greeting. Jaxson frowned deeply and started to snarl as the nurse was trying to remove some of the equipment from the area. "Mr. Upton," the woman exclaimed before turning to Lukas. "Your brother is impatient and spoiled. The doctor will be here shortly to remove the breathing apparatuses. He will simply have to be patient." The section nurse had unnaturally white skin and jet-black hair. She saucily rolled her eyes and twisted her hips as she pushed the machine out. She turned and snapped the curtains closed with such force that both Lukas and Jax cringed.

Lukas handed the whiteboard and marker to his brother, then dragged a chair closer.

Jaxson held up the board with the words 'Oct 15' and a question mark. Lukas nodded. Jaxson emitted a sound that sounded like a strangled groan. He'd been out of commission for more than 3 weeks.

His throat continued to itch but the mean nurse threatened to have his hands strapped down if he didn't leave the breathing tube alone. On the board he wrote, "Lee."

Lukas wondered if he should tell his brother about his conversation with Lee and his suspicion that she was hiding something. He decided his brother needed to know as much as possible to protect himself. "I talked to Lee last night," He replied. Lukas paused to gauge his brother's reaction. Jaxson raised his eyebrows in surprise, then nodded, encouraging Lucas to continue.

"Pop and I ran into her when we left last night. She was trying to convince the nurse to let her see you. Pop wanted to send her packing, but I thought you might want to see her." Lukas paused, and Jaxson nodded. "I gave her permission and asked her to call me when she left you and let me know how you were. We talked about you for a while "

He stopped when Jaxson's face fell. On the board, he wrote 'and?'

Lukas signed and continued, "I asked her why she was here. After I signed her in, the nurse at the station said she had called almost every other day for the last two weeks to see if you could have visitors. It was dumb luck that she decided to come in when she did. She told me on the phone that she simply needed to see for herself that you were okay, but she didn't say why."

Jaxson frowned, then growled when they were interrupted by the return of the nurse followed by the doctor. "Good news, Mr. Upton, the doctor is here to remove the tube and move you out of my ward." Her smile was sharp and her tone sarcastic. Both Lukas and the attending physician wondered what could have happened to cause such animosity.

The nurse began to prep for the procedure. Lukas wondered if Jaxson should be sedated and posed the question to the doctor. Jaxson shook his head violently adding a big 'no' to his whiteboard. The doctor appeared to want to offer a different opinion, but a stern look from the nurse stifled that thought. She pulled the bed remote out of the little pouch on the side of the bed and roughly reclined the bed to a full horizontal position. Jaxson groaned in pain with tears welling fell in his eyes, causing Lukas to jump to his feet in anger.

"Get a new nurse. I don't care how obnoxious my severely injured brother behaves. I will not stand for this kind of treatment." Lucas fought the urge to yell, but both the doctor and nurse responded quickly with fear in their eyes. Lukas was a tall, muscular man and cut a naturally imposing figure in his tailored suits. The nurse and her nasty attitude immediately left the curtained area where Jaxson's bed was.

"I apologize, to you both. I will make sure to talk to her and her supervisor about her behavior." The doctor stuck his head out of the curtain and yelled for another nurse who scrambled in without making eye contact with anyone.

She and the doctor quickly pulled together what they needed for the relatively short but very painful procedure. Lukas took the seat at the front of the bed trusting neither the doctor nor the nurse not to purposefully harm his brother. The entire ordeal took a little over an hour. Jaxson gagged several times, but like the Marine he was, he suffered through it without needing to stop. Lukas wasn't sure how he was able to do it, but he did it. Once it was all done, the doctor announced that Jaxson probably wouldn't talk naturally for a week or so, then let them know that Jaxson would be moved to a private room at some point later in the day. Another, much friendlier acting nurse brought Jaxson his lunch of hot broth, room temperature Jell-O and a cup of ice chips

Jaxson was burned over half the back side of his body with the worst burns occurring on his right side. His right arm was a real mess, burned and broken in three places. The right side of his torso, hip and thigh were burned to the point where skin grafts were definitely in the cards as part of his rehabilitation. Jaxson was still on the morphine drip, but his eyes were clearer, and he was more alert than Lukas had expected.

With the nurses and doctors gone, Jaxson pushed the tray of bland food aside and grab his board for writing, "What day?" He then turned it toward his brother with frantic eyes.

"Tuesday", Lucas reply. "When is Lee coming back? Is she coming back?" Jaxson nodded and wrote "Friday" on his board. He rolled his eyes in an exaggerated fashion. Lukas laughed and said "Perhaps this is for the best. It'll give you a chance to think about what you want to say to her." Lukas sat down and leaned back in the chair waiting to see how Jaxson reacted to that. Then he added, "I believe she has something that she is hiding, but I don't have any idea what it could be, Jaxson."

Jaxson stared off into the distance. His eyes flickered around as he thought about their visit. Lee seemed very uncomfortable and she was acting a bit strangely, even given how things ended between them. Initially, Jaxson had written her jitteriness off as a function of their long absence from one another. But perhaps there was more to it than that.

A new crew of nurses showed up a few hours later to move Jaxson to his new room. The move caused Jaxson quite a bit of pain, so they gave him a double dose of morphine that quickly put him to sleep. Lukas waited nearby until he was sure his brother was fully asleep before going in search of his brother's doctor.

The small thin man was re-reading a chart in a small alcove. He looked troubled, sitting on the edge of a worn blue chair. He jumped when Lukas cleared his throat. "Sorry to interrupt," Lucas said, "the nurse at the desk told me you were over here."

The doctor closed the file and shoved it under a stack of pages. After laying his hand on top of the pile, the doctor stood and turned to face Lukas. He stood a good 6 inches shorter than Lukas and had to crane his neck to look directly into Lukas' face.

"Sorry," he revealed, "I'd like to talk to you about my brother."

When Ava had been born, the brothers had taken steps to ensure they were legally able to speak on each other's behalf in medical emergencies. Lukas had always assumed Jaxson would be the first to need this - but because of his military service overseas, not because of some domestic terrorist. The doctor had been made aware of the living will as soon as Jaxson was brought in. He smartly gave Lukas is full attention. "What are the chances that Jaxson will have full use of his right arm and leg?" Lukas motioned toward the chairs, taking the one nearest where they stood. He waited for the doctor to sit before continuing. "He is committed to his military career and will fight to get back to it."

The doctor sighed. In fact, he had been working on Jaxson's treatment plan when Lukas came over. He leaned over and pulled the file out from the bottom of the stack. For the next two hours, the doctor laid out his proposed treatment plan with Lukas. His plan was to save as much of the skin and muscle as they could, but it would not guarantee a full return all of Jaxson's motor skills.

"Jaxson will never accept anything less than a full recovery." Lucas thought for a moment and then said a quick, silent prayer for the rehabilitation staff that was going to have to suffer through Jaxson's overwhelming work ethic.

Lukas thanked the doctor for his time and the frank conversation. He looked at his watch and paused; he needed to pick up Ava soon. He walked back to his brother's room to check on him before heading out. He made a mental list of things his brother was going to need and wondered how they were going to make it through this.

5

B y Friday morning, Jaxson had gone into full grumpy bear mode. He wouldn't allow anyone shave his face and had taken to growling and snarling at anyone who came too close. His voice was coming back but he tired quickly. Unable to do the things he wanted, he was supremely annoyed – and annoying. He'd run off two more nurses, who'd both declared they weren't being paid enough to deal with Jax's abuse. Lukas finally paid to bring in private nurses that were compensated well to deal with his brother's bad attitude. Ava was the only one that didn't suffer

Jaxson's wrath and the nurses enjoyed the peace that came with the little girl's daily afternoon visits.

Lunch was served and for once he ate it willingly. Once the dishes were cleared and he was alone, Jaxson forced himself to relax. He was scheduled for a session with his dermatologist, but he'd canceled hoping against hope that Lee would return. She may have been skittish and jumpy, but she'd never been one to break her word. Jaxson fought the urge to fall asleep when he heard Lee's voice from the hallway, low and stern.

"I need you both to be on your best behavior while we are here. Understood?"

There was a heartbeat or two of silence. Then came a child's voice. "French fries?" she asked. Jaxson was sure the voice belonged to a little girl.

He paused and wondered to himself – *was this what she was hiding? A husband? Kids?* He closed his eyes and tried to picture her hands in his mind. Jaxson couldn't remember a ring, but that didn't mean anything. He tried to be patient and wait for Lee to come in but failed before thirty seconds could pass.

"Lee!" he croaked out as loudly as he could manage. She peeked around the door, surprise and concern written plainly on her face. Just below her two smaller heads peeked in as well. The sight was rather comical, and Jaxson barked out a scratchy laugh. Lee scowled and stood in the doorway, straightening her suit jacket. Shyly, the two children, a young girl and an even younger little boy followed her, though they stood as close to her legs as they could without her picking them up.

The children were very young. The girl was older, with a mess of shoulder length jet black braids. She looked like Lee, had her mother's medium brown skin and wide brown eyes. The child's nose and mouth must have been inherited from her father, though. Jaxson thought the features looked strangely familiar, but he dismissed that idea immediately. Having only been around Ava he had no clue how old the pretty little girl could be.

The boy was a different matter entirely. He had straight black hair and light green eyes and sucked his thumb with a strange intensity. The little boy must have taken all his looks from his father. He looked nothing like Lee. In fact, if he hadn't seen the child clinging to Lee so intensely, he would have never guessed he belonged to her.

"Hello, Jaxson," she said quietly. She couldn't maintain eye contact and she seemed to focus on everything in the room but Jaxson's face. "I hope you don't mind that I brought the children. Their school was only open for half a day today, and I couldn't find anyone to watch them with such short notice. I just forgot." She added quickly, before he could say anything.

He waved away her concern with his good hand and motioned the three to move closer. Lee pulled one of the chairs closer to the left side of the bed and reached back to pull the little girl's next to it. She turned to the little boy who was still standing by the door trying his best to blend into the wallpaper. The smile Lee gave the little boy made Jax long for the time when she looked at him with such love.

"Come on Dee", she said softly. Lee tried to wave to him, persuade him come to her. But the little girl was not so patient. She jumped down from the chair and grabbed her brother's hand and dragged him to their mother.

"Stop being such a big baby, Dimitri." She pushed the boy the last foot, depositing him at his mother's feet.

Lee gave her daughter an exasperated look of motherly displeasure and picked up the little boy and sat him gently on her lap. She tried to look apologetic, but Lee's fussing over the dust on the boy's pants caused the truly adorable girl's eyes to roll once again.

Jaxson chuckled at the scene unfolding in front of him. He'd never considered Lee as a mother.

She's been very much against having children while they were together. She came from a large extended family, Jaxson recalled, and she cherished her quiet and privacy. *Clearly that had changed*, he figured. He tried to lift his head to see if she was wearing a ring, but without raising the head of the bed he couldn't see a thing from that angle.

"I wonder if you can help me with something," he asked the little girl. She slid off the chair warily and walked the short distance to be closer to the bed but didn't get close enough for him to touch her. "My hand is in a cast over here and I can't reach the remote from the bed. Think you can grab it for me and bring it to my good hand?" He held up his cast for the child to see. She turned to her mother, and getting a nod, she skipped to the other side of the bed.

"Yep. That's it," he said and held out his good hand. She placed the remote in his hand with more gentleness than he'd anticipated and slowly raised himself to a sitting position. The shift caused him to grimace more than once. Lee stood up to help reposition the pillows under his head and leg.

"Should I get a nurse," she asked when she noticed him breaking out in a thin film of sweat along his hairline and upper lip.

"No," he growled. Her eyebrows raised in shock and then her mouth pursed dismay, so he added

"I'm a Marine. We can handle a bit of pain. There, see all is fine."

Something he didn't recognize flashed across her face, but as quickly as it appeared, the look was gone. Her eyes had cooled, and that single, perfectly groomed brow arched again. Jaxson wondered what he'd said to cause that look and silently vowed to never do it again.

Lee resumed her seat, placing Dimitri back in her lap. The little girl eyed him warily. She too had noticed the change in her mom's demeanor. She backed away slowly but didn't walk back to the other side of the bed. Yet.

"Were you in a car accident," the little girl asked without preamble.

"No. No, I wasn't," Jaxson said stumbling over his words. He looked to Lee for some guidance, unsure of how to explain what happened.

Lee gave Jaxson a knowing smile and turned to the girl. "Jaxson was hurt by the bad man that blew up the building downtown."

"The terrorists!" she asked, eyes wide in awe and admiration.

"What do you know about terrorists?" Lee asked in horror.

The girl blushed. "Ms. Carson had a newspaper and I read it. The story was on the cover, so I didn't actually touch her stuff," she murmured.

Lee rolled her eyes then closed them, taking several deep breaths. She opened her mouth to respond but it was Jaxson that exclaimed, "You read a newspaper article?"

The little girl smiled proudly. "Yes, sir"

"How old you are," Jaxson added unable to hide his surprise.

"I'm four and a half," she boasted, "and I could read when I was two. Mommy says I'm too smart for my own good, but I like being smart."

"I'm impressed," Jaxson reply, and she gifted him with a wide smile.

And from there Jaxson and the children were the best of friends.

The highly intelligent little girl and Jaxson had a heated debate on the amount of money the tooth fairy should leave followed closely by which brand had the best gum to blow one's bubbles. Lee and Dimitri were amused by the exchanges but stayed mostly quiet. After about an hour or so, everyone was growing tired. Jaxson and the kids traded yawns with odd regularity, so Lee finally declared an end to the visit. She told the kids to get their things together and get ready to go home.

"It was nice to meet you. I don't think I ever heard your name," Jaxson called out to the little girl.

"I'm Jack," she replied to the stunned Jaxson as she walked out of the room with Lee to close on her heels.

"Wait for me at the elevator, but do not touch anything," Lee said to the kids with one eye on the kids and the other on Jaxson as she waited for him to ask.

"Your daughter's name is Jack," he asked amused.

Lee smiled and chuckled, "Yep, named her Jack after her father." Before Jaxson could say anything, Lee added, "I'll bring her back on Sunday. She doesn't know who you are, so we can tell her together. I'll come back tomorrow and explain to everyone. Goodbye, Jaxson."

Without another word and without looking back to see Jaxson's slack-jawed reaction, Lee headed out to elevator bank. Jaxson couldn't breathe, not until he heard the elevator's bell announcing its arrival on their floor. He'd considered calling them all back in and demanding an explanation, but he was tired, and his brain was not processing the latest dramatic turn in his life. But one thing was clear. Lukas was right. Lee had indeed been hiding something. Something major!

Lee made it to the car and said a prayer that Jaxson was still too injured to follow her. She had dropped a huge bombshell in his lap, then run away like a skittish mouse. She'd thought she was ready to discuss what had happened between them and the ultimate result – their daughter – but she thought wrong. She needed more time and as she strapped Dimitri into his car seat, she prayed for the strength to see this through.

6

As promised, Lee returned the next day. Lukas and Jaxson were in the middle of a loud, heated argument.

"Get out, Lukas," Jaxson snarled when he spied Lee hovering in the doorway. The fear and indecision on Lee's face had him struggling to get up from the bed, murderous rage etched on his reddened face.

Luke turned and frowned. "Now is not a good time, Lee," he said through clinched teeth. "Please, come back later. "

"If anyone is leaving, it's you, big brother." Jaxson tried to sit up and grimaced in pain.

Lee was torn between walking away as Lukas has asked and staying put to make sure Jaxson didn't do serious damage to himself. Lukas rolled his eyes and grabbed his coat and left without saying another word. Lee watched him go but wanted to ask him to stay. Belatedly, she realized she really wanted him to be there for the coming conversation. But she recognized the look on Jaxson's face, and it didn't bode well for her. Jaxson had always had a fierce temper and something his brother had said had piqued it. She let Lukas go, and turned back toward Jaxson. She nearly smiled. The face staring back at her was exactly the one Jack gave her when she had lost her temper.

He was sitting somewhat upright. His casted leg was raised in a brace. His arm had been hoisted over his head. He was wearing a compression top and one sleeve on his exposed left thigh. Jaxson looked pissed off and uncomfortable. Lee sighed and walked in, dragging the chair next to the bed.

She'd just sat down and crossed her legs when Jaxson blurted out, "Are you sure the little girl is mine?"

Time stopped. Lee couldn't breathe. She was instantly enraged. Rather than give this asshole of a man a piece of her mind, she jumped up grabbing her purse off the floor and headed for the door.

"Please don't leave, Lee." Something about Jaxson's voice made her stop despite her anger, but she didn't turn back to him.

"I'm sorry. I didn't mean it like that. Please, come back." Lee weighed her options. In the end, her daughter needed for her to see this conversation to completion. And she'd try her best not to smother the gravely injured man that was her daughter's father with his own pillow. She slowly made her way back into the room but didn't sit. She cocked a single shapely eyebrow and waited for him to say something else stupid.

"Why didn't you tell me about the baby," he asked quietly afraid to break eye contact. Lee looked like she was ready to break his other arm and leg. He didn't blame her. Lukas was concerned that Leigh may have been after something and was pushing him to request a blood test when Lee arrived. The request had infuriated Jaxson and he didn't have any more sense than to turn around and make the request of Lee. He groaned inwardly.

"I wanted to, but you left to fight a war." She replied simply. She placed her purse in the chair and walked over to the window and looked out. "You didn't leave any forwarding information and the cell number you'd given me was disconnected, so I tried to get a message to you, but the military said you couldn't be contacted directly. Instead, I was to give them my message and they would pass it on to you. I didn't think that was the best way to find out the woman you'd so heartlessly left behind was pregnant." She turned back to him and added, "Do you?"

"Lee", he started, before closing his mouth and trying to look away from her. She was right. He had heartlessly abandoned her. But she didn't have any clue of the real reason why. And he wasn't ready to explain himself to her just yet.

She walked back around the bed, her eyes boring a hole in his face. It was obvious she waited a long time to get this off her chest. "Initially I was going to go Kenya and be with my mom and sister, but I thought that would be unnecessarily cruel, to put so much distance between you and your child. So, I figured I'd wait until you came back. But you never did. I left message after message for you to contact me. But you never stepped foot on a base in North Carolina again, did you?"

Lee paused to give Jaxson a chance to answer. But there was nothing for him to say. She was right. He'd jumped at every assignment that came his way. After his last tour ended, he was offered an opportunity to teach on the West Coast. He took it without hesitation.

"My guess is, you ran off to some new job and new life, not wanting to run into me after how big of an asshole you'd been. And in your cowardice, you've missed out on four years of your daughter's life." Lee's bottom lip trembled as her breath hitched and she fought her tears.

Jaxson felt sick to the stomach. Still unable to make eye contact with Lee, he spoke somewhere to a point over her shoulder, "Does she know anything about me? I mean, what have you told her?"

Lee gave him a sour smile. "She knows about you. I didn't lie to my daughter when she asked me about her father. I was so angry with you that I burned all your pictures, so I wasn't lying when I told her I don't have any. She doesn't know that you are her father, because she's never seen you before."

Jaxson nodded. "Do you think she can handle it if we tell her," he asked, finally daring to look at Lee. She was still furious. Her emotions always were on full display on her face. Lukas didn't have to worry about Lee's ulterior motives. From the looks of it, she'd rather leave and never return. Jaxson was worse than an asshole. He was a coward.

"Jacinta is a genius. Like an actual certified genius. I have the paperwork to prove it. She can handle just about anything. Just be aware that you will have to answer a lot of questions. She excels at inappropriate and uncomfortable questions." Lee laughed quietly to herself. Her daughter rated off the charts in every test the doctors have found to give her so far. She had a vocabulary larger than many adults. Lee had resigned herself to merely keeping up with her precious little Jack.

Jaxson was silent for a solid minute. Lee couldn't know it, but he wondered if knowing him was the right thing for the little girl. Lee was probably a fantastic mother. Did he really need to mess things up for either of them?

Lee's voice snapped him out of his internal debate "I want her to know you. She is currently obsessed with science. Especially chemical composites. I am a CPA. She didn't inherit that madness from me," she said it with a laugh. "I really think it would do both of you some good to get to know each other."

Jaxson smiled. He'd blown up his share of things in his quest for knowledge, as a child and as an adult. "OK," was all he got out before the orderly came to take him to his rehab appointment.

It had been about a month since the blast. His scrambled brains were starting to heal and regaining his mobility in his broken limbs was now his top concern. Unfortunately, the worst burns were on his broken arm and leg, making the progress difficult and excruciating. Plus, Jaxson was an awful patient – willful, stubborn, and impatient with himself. He drove everyone crazy with his need for perfection. As he left Lee and was being wheeled down the hall, he made up his mind to work even harder to get out the hospital, and the staff would have to simply deal.

7

Jaxson would end up spending more than two
months in the hospital. Lee brought the kids
to visit as often as she could. During the first
visit after Jaxson found out Jack was his daughter,
he asked her to sit on the side of bed and talk to
him. Lee hoisted the little girl up and carefully
lowered Jack on the bed then sat in a chair by the
window pulling her little boy into her lap.

"You're my daddy, aren't you," Jack asked with
a big smile but without any other preamble or
warning.

Jaxson stiffened. He had planned to ease her into
the conversation, but as Lee had warned him, little

Jack loved to jump directly to the hard questions. He steeled himself before answering. "I am. How did you know?" He wasn't sure he wanted to know the answer to that question.

"You look like me" she replied as she fidgeted with the sheets on the bed. Jaxson took her small hands in his. "How come you broke up with my mommy? Don't you love her?"

Lee jumped out of the chair, nearly dropping the little boy onto the floor. "Jacinta! That is completely inappropriate." She shifted the little boy on her hip before moving closer to Jack and leaning down. "We discussed this," she whispered angrily. "You must think before you ask someone personal questions!"

She turned to Jaxson and mouthed "I told you so," and rolled her eyes before returning to her seat. Jaxson wondered how to answer and decided absolute honesty was best. For all of them. He hadn't told Lee this much, but then — Lee had not asked. "I'm a Marine. In the U.S. military. I went on a mission and couldn't tell your mom where I was. And, I hated to leave her, but that was the life I signed up for when I enlisted. Do you know that word, enlisted? You probably do. Anyway, I didn't think she wanted the life of a military wife, so I never came back to North Carolina. I swear I didn't know about you, and I never ever intended to hurt you or your mom. I promise."

Jack nodded, but seemed intent on thinking of her next question, instead of blurting out. Jaxson smiled. Jack gave her mom a look. Jaxson tried to read it, but then Jack asked in a small, suddenly very childlike voice, "Are you going away again when you get better?"

Jaxson looked at Lee who was doing her best to look anywhere else - out the window, at the ceiling, down the hallway behind her - but not at her daughter and ex-boyfriend.

"I don't know. But you and your mom will always be able to find me, and I'll always answer when you call me. I want to be your dad, Jack." Jaxson smiled and hoped his words made sense. He had very little experience with children; mostly he spent time with his niece who was younger and less gifted as the girl fidgeting next to him.

Jack leaned forward on her knees and hugged her new dad, then pulled away abruptly with a deep frown on her face. "What about Dimitri? Can you be Dimitri's dad too? My grandma says boys need a father."

Jaxson and Jack turned and stared at the little boy who had been diligently playing with his mom's phone until he heard his name. He dropped his mom's phone to the floor and did his best to burrow into Lee's side.

"He's really shy," Jack said with an adult-looking roll of her eyes that perfectly mimicked her mother's exasperated face. Jaxson tried not to laugh. She leaned close to his ear and whispered, "His real mommy died and now my mommy is his mommy. That's why we don't look-alike. He never had a daddy." Jaxson's eyes flittered between Lee, Dimitri, and Jack. Lee was busy trying to calm Dimitri who'd reacted badly to being noticed. "Dimitri" Jaxson said, adding as much bass and authority in his voice as he used when commanding a squadron.

The boy immediately quit fighting with his mother, freezing in place.

"Dimitri," Jaxson repeated, adding a tough warning to his voice.

The child straightened up on his mother's lap. His eyes went wide as he slid down to stand on the floor, but he still didn't speak.

"Jacinta, please go sit next to your mother so I can talk to your brother."

Lee stood and picked up Jack with worry, fear, and warning in her eyes. She placed Jack on the floor, picked Dimitri up and placed him on the bed. She hesitated in case Dimitri tried to bolt. He didn't like strangers and had no sense of self-preservation when trying to get away. But he simply settled in, not as close as fearless Jack, but more comfortable than she'd seen him in a long while. Lee sat back down but was on the edge of her seat in case her baby boy needed her.

Jaxson and Dimitri eyed each other wearily. Dimitri was nervously gnawing on his fingers and he still had not spoken a single word. Jaxson was sure Dimitri could talk, but he'd clearly suffered a trauma of some kind. His niece Ava was as fearless as Jack – she had no concept of strangers. Jaxson made a mental note to find out more. "How are you, sir?" Jaxson asked in the same heavy voice.

"Fine," came a very small softly-pitched voice. The word came out low and mumbled, spoken around the two fingers in his mouth.

"Young man, please remove your hand from your mouth when you speak." Jaxson wasn't sure how he knew, but he used the same tone he used on his students – the one that had earned him his reputation as an unyielding hard-ass in the classroom. Lee looked like she was going to strangle him, but he kept his focus on the little boy.

Dimitri immediately pulled his hand from his mouth. He and Jaxson smiled at each other. Lee was dumbfounded. She's been trying for weeks to get Dimitri to take his hand out of his mouth and talk to no avail. Jaxson manages the task in a single conversation. Jack's knowing giggle pulled her out of her musing wonderment.

Jaxson ignored mother and daughter for the moment and focused on the adorable little boy sitting beside him.

Dimitri started to put his hand in his mouth and caught himself. Lee could barely handle the change in the little boy in such a short amount of time. She'd been so focused on bringing Jaxson and Jack together, but she didn't once think about how any of this would affect Dimitri. Lee felt like a heel. She hadn't given a single thought to the little boy she'd raised since her best friend's death at the hands of Dimitri's father.

Dimitri smiled and said, loud and clear, "yes, sir."

Jaxson smiled, and Lee wondered if Jaxson knew just what he was getting into. Dimitri was quiet and introspective by nature – the exact opposite of Jack. But he could be a handful when excited or overwhelmed. Another thought crossed Lee's mind –Jaxson had made some big promises to Jack and she'd hold him accountable. Jack was brilliant, but she didn't know the meaning of forgive and forget. Lee made a mental note to talk to Jaxson about watching what he said to her in the future.

And so, it came to pass that the day before Jaxson's scheduled release from the hospital, Lee and the kids arrived to find Jaxson in yet another heated argument with his brother and father.

"I'm not moving into another hospital," Jaxson yelled loudly enough to be heard from the hallway. Lee hesitated, but the kids took off full speed into their dad's room. Jack and Dimitri had been introduced to their Uncle Lukas and grandfather as soon as Jaxson could arrange to have them all visit him at the same time. And despite some uncomfortable questioning by Jack, Pop and Lukas welcomed both kids to the family. And Jack simply adored her new cousin, Ava.

Lee hovered at the door as Lukas lifted Dimitri and set him on the bed. Jack played with Ava, helping the younger girl with a large piece puzzle and identified the animals depicted on the wooden pieces. "Everything okay," she asked seeing the frowns on the men's faces. "Should I take the kids for a snack while you work things out?"

Lukas nodded and was about to speak when Jaxson yelled, "No one is going anywhere." Dimitri scrambled off the bed, hitting the concrete very hard. He was chewing on his hand nervously as he quickly scooted over to his mom. Lee picked the boy up and snuggled him close.

"Damn it, Lee. Put that boy down!" Jaxson growled.

Lee raised a single eyebrow and said, in a voice that no one would dare to argue with, "If you yell at me or anyone else in this hospital in front of these children again, you won't be getting out of the hospital for another six weeks."

Jack heard her mom's tone and paused looking between her parents. Deciding things weren't too bad she and Ava went back to their puzzles.

Jaxson, Lukas, and Pop looked properly contrite. "Now," Lee continued, "What is the problem? Quietly."

Jaxson snarled, but held his tone steady and replied, "My brother is sending me to another hospital to continue my convalescence. I'm simply refusing to go."

Lee looked around the room before asking. "Where do you want to go?"

"Home," Jaxson said simply.

Lee blinked then frown. "Jaxson be reasonable," She huffed. "Next option?"

It was Jaxson's turn to huff. "I am not going to another hospital, Lee."

"Will you please be reasonable, Jaxson. Where is your home? If you go home, who will take care of you? I mean, is your house one story or two? Can you afford around-the-clock care? And what is the military suggesting?" She fired the questions in such rapid succession that all three men were speechless for several seconds.

This was the Lee that Jaxson remembered. Pragmatic and logical to the bitter end. He refused to budge an inch on the matter, so he stayed stubbornly silent. Lukas and Pop exchanged amused looks. Lukas refused to say anything.

Pop gave Jaxson a victorious smile before turning to Lee. "He lives in California in a fourth-floor walkup. He has no one to take care of him but me and he won't come home with me. He cannot afford a round-the-clock care. And the stubborn jackass won't take the money from his brother. And the military has said he needs to report to the V.A. facility in San Diego, if he does not make other arrangements."

Lee put Dimitri down and he scrambled over to play with Ava and Jack. She turned to Jaxson, her face full of sternness and impatience. "Jaxson Upton, you have been a pain in the behind to every person you've come in contact with since the explosion. I can't imagine what you've been through, but you have to accept that you need help." She used the voice she used with the children when they were on the verge of a meltdown. "You know what options are available and you need to pick one. You cannot take care of yourself. Accept it and move on."

The room was silent. Jaxson pouted, Lukas stood with his mouth gapped open and Pop smirked. Lee rolled her eyes and sighed while taking a seat. This could go on for a while. To be honest she had no dog in this fight, and she once again considered taking the kids on that walk after all.

"I can take care of daddy." Jack stood next to her father, concerned with fear on her little face.

"Jack," Lee said. She pulled the little girl close, putting her hands over the child's mouth and smiling to hide the fear of Jaxson moving into their house. "Mommy works and you're too little. We can't nurse your daddy back to health."

"But..." the words died as Jack began to cry. She pulled herself together enough to whisper, "I don't want daddy to go away again."

"We'd still visit him in the new hospital. It would be just like it is now." She hugged the child, who was clearly on her way to hysterics. A high 'IQ' didn't negate all innate four-year-old tendencies. Lee lifted her to her lap and cradled her.

"Well," Lukas said quietly. "The... um... V.A. hospital Jaxson is going to is in California and kids aren't allowed."

The look Lee gave Lukas could melt steel. Jack truly lost it at that point. Jaxson threw the box of tissues that had been sitting on the bedside table, hitting his brother in the back of the head. Lukas grabbed the box off the floor and Jaxson widened his eyes in a look that said fix it.

"If Jaxson were to come home with you, I'd be willing to pay for the equipment and a nurse for the daytime hours. I realize this would be some additional work for you, you know with the kids and all, so maybe a maid too?"

Lee glared at him over Jack's head. Until he'd said that she would have politely declined to have Jaxson anywhere near her house. It was one thing to facilitate Jack's relationship with her father but certainly that didn't include taking his burned and broken body home with her? She sighed.

"Pop, can you take the kids to get ice cream or something in the shop?" she asked. Dimitri, who'd been completely oblivious to anything but his sister's loud wails, smiled at the mention of ice cream.

"Sure. But Jack can't have snacks until she finishes her cry." That worked just as he'd intended. Her head popped up and she fought back the sob. She slid off her mother's lap and took three tissues from the box Lukas was still holding. She took Dimitri's hand and led him over to the door to wait for Pop, who had the money to procure the promised snacks.

"Lukas, you and Ava should go to. Lee and I need to talk." Jaxson said as evenly as he could manage. He frowned with the effort, knowing how he would be imposing on an already very strained relationship. It was clear she wasn't exactly excited about the idea of having him in her home. But he, surprisingly to even himself, was.

Lee and Jaxson waited for the men to escort the kids out of the room. Lee closed the door and leaned against it. Watching Jaxson through almost closed eyes she took several deep breaths trying to steady her running mind. She was near to hyperventilating. When she opened her eyes, they were wet with unshed tears.

"Lee," Jaxson started. He wasn't sure where the urge came from, but he wanted to hold and comfort her. He had long ago convinced himself that he was totally over her, so why kissing Lee's tears away was even a fleeting thought, he couldn't understand.

"I don't want you in my house," she said, and her voice cracked. The tears fell freely but she didn't move or make another sound. Lee didn't know what else to say and Jaxson's face blushed profusely. Finally, she moved away from the door and almost collapsed into the chair.

When she and Jaxson had been together, she'd had a definite order to her life. Almost painfully so.

She had a plan for everything. The slightest change in her carefully laid out world would often send her into a tailspin. Lee hated surprises and needed a schedule for even the most mundane activities. They had some of their most heated arguments when Jax would want to do something spontaneously that interrupted her carefully laid plans.

Jaxson had assumed the kids would have killed that need for strict structure, but no. And now she was fighting hysterics right in front of him. But was the problem him or the possible disruption to her order? He resolved to stay silent until she worked out in her mind what she needed to say.

Counting the seconds in his head, Jaxson figured at least three minutes had passed before Lee trust herself speak again. Her voice was thick with the emotion and pain she'd buried over the last five years. "When you left, I was devastated. Then I found out I was pregnant. And I wanted to die. How could I raise a baby with a man who didn't care enough about me to tell me he was leaving?" Jaxson wanted to interrupt her, but her glare was enough to keep him silent. "I seriously contemplated getting an abortion," she continued. "We both know I should never have been someone's mother. No child should have to suffer with such a neurotic nutcase for a parent. But when the time came, I couldn't do it. And I've never regretted it." She paused again, getting her thoughts together again. She picked at an invisible string on her jeans and didn't look at him when she said, "I'd move heaven and hell for those kids, and I suppose you qualify as my own personal hell. So, you can move in with us, but you have to stay the hell away from me. I can forgive you for Jack and Dimitri's sakes, but I will never forget the way you treated me. Is that clear?"

Jaxson could do nothing more than nod. Her words burned a hole in his soul. She nodded in return then stood and went back to the door to find three happy, but very dirty children and two baffled men walking down the corridor. Lee was certain Jack had ice cream in both of her ponytails. Ava's face was almost completely covered in a sticky blue sauce and Dimitri's shirt looked almost tie-dyed.

"What on earth happened to you three," Lee asked as Jack skipped up to her, smiling widely. And yes, she confirmed silently, that was definitely ice cream in her baby girl's hair. She frowned inwardly at the thought of having to wash Jack's hair later that night.

"Uncle Lukas said I could have an ice cream cone, but it was melting too fast. Dimitri got it all over his shirt. Grandpa and Ava had Jell-O, but she's not really good at feeding herself. The Jell-O melted and got all over her face." Finished with her tale, Jack scooted passed her mom to check on her dad.

Still reeling from the tale, Lee barely registered when Pop said "They've turned off the AC in the cafeteria for the winter, so it's pretty warm in there. This, um, warm snap has surprised us all." He reached out and patted her shoulder before turning to Ava and Dimitri. "Come on kiddos, let's go and say goodbye."

They walked in the room, leaving Lukas and Lee in the hallway.

"Everything worked out," Lukas asked tentatively. The flash of anger in Lee's eyes was quickly covered with resignation.

"Yes, even though I'm fairly certain I've been set up." She said tersely. "But I'm willing to give it a try it for Jack's sake." She used the thumb and forefinger of her right hand to massage the bridge of her nose between her eyes. A headache was growing quickly across her cheeks to her ears. This was nothing like how she thought the day would have gone. It was too much.

Lukas sighed in relief. "I'm glad. I've ordered the items Jaxson needs for his recovery; they just need to know where to deliver it. I honestly thought you'd talk him into going home with Pop." He pulled out his phone and opened it to her contact info. "If you'll add your address, I'll have the guys come and set up that space."

Lee's head popped up. She hadn't thought about where to put him. She and the kids had just moved into their house less than six months ago, and not all the rooms were furnished. The dining room was probably the best idea. The room was near the bathroom on the first floor and was very spacious. The table and chairs she ordered where to be delivered in the next two weeks but that could easily be stored in garage. She nodded, accepting what Lukas said and decided not to pursue the issue any further.

"Daddy wait until you see my room. And you can help with my science kit. Mom isn't good at science. She made one of glass test tubes explode and she cut herself." Jack caught herself and her cheeks reddened.

"Jack, help your brother get ready to go, please," Lee interrupted before Jack could tell Jaxson something else embarrassing. She turned back to Lukas and rolled her eyes.

"I'm not sure if my brother said this but he really appreciates this. He absolutely adores the kids." Lukas stopped talking abruptly, afraid he may say too much and make an already tense situation worse.

Lee cocked an eyebrow. "The kids adore him too but make no mistake, if you hadn't said anything about him going to a child-free hospital in front of Jack, he'd be going somewhere else," she said in a harsh whisper.

Lukas took a step back, surprised by the venom in her voice. He wondered exactly what Jaxson left out in his retelling of their breakup that would warrant this kind of response from the generally even-tempered woman. Lukas could only imagine. His brother had been running from real life for years now. It seems like life has finally caught up with him. Lukas tried not to smile – he knew Lee would think he was laughing at her and not the fact that his little brother was about to get the harshest wake-up call of his reckless life.

She gave him a weary smile and asked, "so let's discuss this maid you're paying for the next year?"

8

The next morning Lukas and a crew of five muscular men arrived at Lee's house. In what should've been her formal dining room, the men cleared out the boxes of dishes and glassware, carefully relocating them to the garage. The dining room had beautiful antique French doors that Lee insisted that they remove lest they get broken. The doors were one of the things she loved about the house and she'd be heartbroken if they were damaged in anyway.

In short order, the man had assembled a hospital bed and a makeshift rehab area with weights, and exercise bike, and a standalone set of stairs. They added handrails to the downstairs bathroom and a ramp to the front of the house that Lukas assured her would be easy to remove once it was no longer needed. Jaxson was being released but he still had a myriad of doctors' appointments and several surgeries ahead of him. Jaxson was expected to be with Lee and the kids for at least six months, depending on how well his body healed from his surgeries.

Pop showed up after lunch with a grumpy Jaxson. His casted arm was in a sling and his casted leg was propped up in his wheelchair. Lee waited just inside the front door with the kids while Lukas pushed Jaxson up the ramp.

The still bruised and battered man gave Jack and Dimitri a big smile when he crossed the threshold. The kids had been kept busy working on 'welcome home' signs while the workmen were in and out making the house wheelchair accessible for Jaxson. Dimitri would have kept his distance from the strange men and women, but Jack's curiosity would have prompted her asking a thousand questions and getting into trouble, with Dimitri hot on her heels. They proudly held up their signs and bounced around Jaxson and the wheelchair.

Lee grabbed them and pulled them out of the way with a quick word of warning, "let's let your father get comfortable in his new room and then you can tell him all about your signs until dinner."

Jaxson grunted and smiled as Lee followed Lukas and Jaxson to Jaxson's new bedroom. Jack ran forward and locked the wheelchair wheels when they stopped near the bed. Pop quickly shuffled to the side with Jaxson's good arm, leaving Lukas to deal with the cast and burns. It took a couple of tries to maneuver, but they finally got the now growly man in the bed and reasonably comfortable. Lukas ran outside to grab Jaxson's bag from Pop's car, then returned making quick work of putting the few things in the new chest of drawers Lukas had delivered for him. Lukas made a mental note to go by Jaxson's place and get more clothes. Lee wouldn't be happy having to do laundry every couple of days because Jaxson only had four pairs of underwear. But then, he remembered the cleaning service he contracted with. They were scheduled to send a maid over three days a week for the next year and would most likely be forced to deal with Jaxson and his laundry problems.

Lukas realized he'd been daydreaming when he snapped too, and everyone was staring at him. "What?" He asked defensively.

"Where," Jaxson repeated, annoyed. "Is my TV?"

"Oh good... I will bring you one tomorrow. Think you can last that long," Lukas responded with an exasperated roll of his eyes. "Is there anything else I can bring you when I come by tomorrow with the all-important television set?" Lukas reached in his pocket and handed him a cell phone. "Since yours was destroyed in the blast."

Jaxson grabbed the phone with his good hand and laid it in his lap. "Thanks," he mumbled, aware the kids were watching.

"Well, I have a date to get ready for," Pop announced with the bounce on the balls of his feet. Lukas and Jaxson stared at their father in complete shock.

"Is she pretty, grandpa?" Jack asked, then as she remembered what her mom said about personal questions. Her eyes grew wide and she clasped her hands over her mouth with a loud gasp. Pop took no offense, having grown accustomed to Jack's blunt questioning style.

"The lady is gorgeous," Pop replied winking at Jack, who beamed. He kissed her on the head, ruffled Dimitri's unruly curly black hair, slapped Lukas on the shoulder then turned to roll his eyes at Jaxson before happily strolling out the house.

"Did that grouchy old man just wink at a child after announcing he was going on a date?" Lukas tried to put the pieces together in his head, to no avail. He shook his head and glanced at his watch.

He gasped when he realized how late it had gotten. "I better run too."

"You got a big date too?" Jaxson said amused.

"Um, no," Lukas replied curtly. "But if I don't get Ava soon, the babysitter will fillet me.

Lee laughed. And caught Jack mouthing the word.

"Like a fish fillet at the restaurant, Uncle Lukas," she asked frowning at the image in her mind.

"File it away baby girl, and we'll look it up later," Lee cut in, keeping Lukas up from a protracted conversation.

He smiled and nodded, Jack frowned and nodded and wandered out the room with Lukas following. "Call me if you need anything, Lee," he added with a laugh that followed him to the front door. Dimitri ran out as well, most likely following his sister, leaving Lee and Jaxson alone.

Jaxson fidgeted under Lee's unwavering gaze.

"Is this what you wanted," she asked in a low voice. She didn't want to alert the kids to anything amiss.

"I'm not sure I understand..." Jaxson let his words trail off. He knew exactly what she was asking, and she knew it. In truth, he really hadn't planned for things to turn out like this, but he couldn't muster any ill-feelings about it. But he didn't know how he could possibly explain that to Lee that in a way that she would believe.

"Look Lee, this isn't what I wanted, but I won't insult your intelligence - I'm okay with it because it means that I can spend more time with Jack and Dimitri."

Lee looked like she was chewing on his words. Jaxson said a silent prayer that she accepted his words at face value. After several tense seconds, she gave three sharp nods and turned to go.

"Dinner will be at six. Holler if you need anything." She threw her purse over her shoulder as she walked away

Jaxson stared at the empty door, his mind racing. After everyone left the night before, Jaxson tried watching TV, but his mind kept going back to Lee's words. She had been so easy when the kids were around, he'd had no clue the amount of rage she had simmering just below the surface. And he knew he was completely to blame for it.

9

L ee had always been perfect for Jaxson. She was generally calm and cool and always under control. It took quite a bit to push her over the edge. She'd been the perfect complement to Jaxson's impetuous nature. He always leapt before looking and spoke without thinking. And when once he realized he was having serious, 'forever-like' feelings for her, he bolted from the relationship. Jaxson volunteered for the first overseas assignment that came up. His chosen profession and industry were dangerous and often required extended absences. Jaxson told himself this was for the better, that he simply didn't want to put Lee through the USMC life. He knew Lee better than she'd thought – in his mind he was doing the right thing for them both. It never occurred to him to tell her about his fears regarding their relationship.

His father had always told him not to trust anyone's emotions and to remember to keep his heart and mind protected. Pop had loved his only wife beyond distraction and never recovered when she committed suicide while Jaxson and Lukas were small boys. His mother had suffered from debilitating depression. Pop finally came clean about her fight with mental illness when Lukas went through a rough patch after the death of his own wife, Emmalyn. Lukas and Em had finally figured out their relationship when Em died giving birth to their daughter. Pop fought like crazy to force Lukas to get help. Not just for baby Ava's sake, but because he recognized the same hopelessness in his son that he'd felt when he'd lost the love of his life. It had taken Pop more than twenty-five years to move on from Margie's death. It wasn't something he'd ever wanted for either of his boys.

Jaxson may have acted like he had a death wish, but he enjoyed his life. But this glimpse into the family he could have had made him seriously question everything he'd thought was true. It hadn't taken long after Lee had come back in his life before Jaxson realized he still had very, very real feelings for her.

Then there was Jacinta. His own little Jack. Jack was so much like him it was uncanny – considering she'd spent so little time around him. And Dimitri was slowly getting used to Jaxson's attention. He still didn't talk very much, but he didn't cling to Lee like a stamp on a letter as much as he'd used to either. Jaxson didn't know the full story behind Dimitri's parents, but Lee was in the process of formally adopting the child and that process was nearing completion.

Jaxson wondered if he could stay here the expected six months without Lee murdering him in his sleep. He felt it was highly unlikely to be honest. He'd always driven her close to insane – and that was part of the fun. The day nurse was slated to begin Monday, and the maid would come on Tuesdays, Wednesdays, and Thursdays. Lee would have plenty of help with the kids and the house, and Lukas had made sure the maid was able to cook on the days she worked. However, for this first weekend it would be only the four of them and Jaxson wasn't sure they'd make it. Lee was just so hurt and enraged. Jaxson laid back on the bed and drifted into a fitful sleep.

It took forty-five minutes, three different encyclopedia volumes and the dictionary to give Jack a satisfactory answer to the origin and meaning of the word "fillet." And of course, that led to a conversation on types of fish, fisheries, production for the market, shipping processes, and the implements used to fillet fish. By the end, Jack had declared filleting to be a bad way to die and took her brother off to her room to color.

Lee leaned back on her bed and started to daydream. Not for the first time since she'd found out she was pregnant, she wondered how different things would be if Jaxson hadn't left her. She'd been utterly heartbroken when she realized Jaxson had gone on deployment without so much as a goodbye. And she'd been near inconsolable when she realized that Jaxson had no intention of coming back to North Carolina at all. This was too much. She couldn't deny that Jack, and even Dimitri, was thrilled at having their new dad living in their home. It bothered her to admit the weakness to herself, let alone anyone else, but she didn't want to become accustomed to having him around again. Because it wouldn't be just her heart getting broken when he decided he'd had enough.

For her part, Jack sensed that her mom was worrying. Several times the night before Jaxson's arrival, she'd tried to convince her mother that everything was going to be okay, but Lee wasn't so sure.

Sighing to herself, Lee sat up and shook herself out of her doldrums. Short break over, Lee stood up and walked down the hall to Jack's bedroom. The kids were knee-deep into building blocks.

"Ok, you two, time for me to cook dinner. Come downstairs and play." Lee helped the kids clean up the mess and they made their way down the noisy steps.

Lee cringed. She wasn't sure if Jaxson was sleep or not. Quietly, she led the kids into the den and whispered, "You can turn on the TV, but be very quiet so you don't disturb your dad." Lee turned to go into the kitchen and found Jaxson in the doorway.

"What are you doing out of bed?" Lee said with a scolding tone then rushing to his side. She helped him over to the sofa and propped his broken leg on a throw pillow she placed on top of the foot stool. "Now that the cast is gone and you have that boot, don't think you can just walk willy-nilly all over town. You just had those skin grafts on your side a week ago. You have to let them heal before you try to move around the house."

"I heard someone was watching cartoons and I wanted in," he replied jovially, winking at the giggling Jack.

Lee rolled her eyes and shuffled back to the kitchen. She chopped and shredded, imagining the onions and potatoes for the Shepard's pie had Jaxson's smug face. She had to laugh at herself. She'd never been an overly emotional person, but Jaxson always seemed to bring out that side of her without even trying.

A little over an hour later, she laid the completed meal out on the small table in her breakfast nook. She went to call Jaxson and the kids to eat. The three were cuddled on the sofa like they'd had a lifetime of comforting each other there, instead of an hour. The picture melted the hurt... if just a little. She almost felt bad breaking up the love fest. Almost.

"Come eat you guys." No one moved. Lee cleared her throat trying to get their attention, but the three merely stared blankly at the screen. Lee growled softly and said "Hey!"

Jaxson turned to look in Lee's direction. She stood there in full displeased mom mode, with hands on her hips. He tried to disentangle the kids and stand, losing his balance and falling over the footstool Lee had propped his leg on.

"Oh my God, Jaxson?" Lee descended on him, checking him for injury and helping him to his feet. "Are you all right?"

"Yes, I'm fine," he replied trying to hide his pain-riddled grimaces.

"Your stitches," she said trying to help him up without putting pressure on his wounds.

"They are fine," he said, embarrassed. He hated being weak and needing help, especially in front of the kids.

"Good grief, you scared me to death," said Lee with a loving tone in her voice. "Your father and brother would never forgive me if I let anything happen you." said Lee. Jaxson and Lee shared a brief familiar moment.

Lee recognized that glance, snapped out of it and turned to tell the kids, "Dinner is ready! And for the love of all that is holy in germs, go wash those grimy hands!"

Jack and Dimitri took the hint and ran to the bathroom. "And you," she said through clenched teeth, "had better be more careful. And answer when I call you! I can't have you getting reinjured on my watch." Certain he was stable on his feet, Lee huffed and stormed off into the kitchen.

Jaxson sighed deeply. He turned slowly and followed Lee's path to the kitchen. He hesitated as Lee was strapping Dimitri to the booster seat. Lee straightened and gave Jaxson an exasperated look that he was really growing very fond of.

Jaxson shrugged and said, "I wasn't sure if I should eat in my room or..." His words trailed off and he gestured toward the table.

"No, daddy," Jack exclaimed, a horrified look on her face. "We don't eat in our bedrooms. That's what causes bugs. Food should be eaten in the designated areas." Lee nodded to add emphasis to the little girl's words.

"Sit down Jaxson, the food is getting cold." Lee said as she fixed plates for Dimitri, then Jack and finally herself. She waited for Jaxson to get situated.

"Some help?" He asked and held up his broken right hand.

Lee winked at Jack and joked, "And your daddy was going to live all by himself. He can't even fix himself a plate of food!" She placed food on his plate in an overly exaggerated fashion, eliciting a giggle from both Jack and Dimitri. "Okay, Jack, Please, bless the food."

Jack folded her hands and in all the seriousness a four-year-old could muster recited the prayer they said every night before dinner.

Jaxson didn't know Lee was at all religious. He wondered what else about her he'd missed. His stomach clenched in fear. This was a torture he deserved.

"Daddy, you eat after the prayer," Jack told him, and he didn't miss the mimicry of Lee's exasperated voice come out of the little girl.

"Yes, ma'am", he replied and dug into the first home cooked meal he'd had in almost a year.

10

Two weeks into their new arrangement, Lee was ready to explode. The nurse and maid consistently moved her things and Lee was late four times trying to find something that wasn't where she would have normally put it. Jack and Dimitri were picking up Jaxson's bad habits and she constantly felt like an outsider to their little club - in her own home. Jaxson had been nothing but polite and even that was grating on her nerves. She hated feeling like a shrew, but she wasn't ready to forgive and forget yet, either.

This particular morning was a certified disaster. It was a Wednesday, so the physical therapist was in Jaxson's room putting him through his morning workout. The doorbell rang just as Lee stuffed the second sandwich she'd made for Jack (having dropped, then stepped on the first) into the cartoon lunchbox that sat empty on the counter. Lee rolled her eyes and headed for the door half lamenting that she would be late again and half wondering who could possibly be at the door so early in the morning. She looked out the decorative glass in her front door to find a man in a black suit shifting from foot to foot and looking very uncomfortable. He was short and bald, and kept reaching up to tug at the collar of his shirt attesting to the crisp morning air. He spied her peering at him and tried to smile.

"Miss Anderson", he said a bit too cheerfully. "I have a letter for you." He held up said letter and waved it around a bit in an effort to pique her interest.

Lee looked to see the children still happily coloring at the nook's table. She unlocked the door, opening it just wide enough for the man to slip his arm in and pass her the letter. She used her foot as a door stop. She took the letter and examined the sender. It was from some law office downtown, but she didn't recognize it. She looked at the man who had inched his way to the edge of the porch and seemed ready to bolt at any second and frowned.

"Um, you've been served ma'am," he said sadly. And then he did, in fact, bolt. Lee threw the door open wide and watched the man run for his car, jump in, and speed off before she could ask any questions.

"Lee," came a concerned voice from somewhere behind her. She turned blindly to find Jaxson standing about ten feet away, his face bunched in an angry frown.

Lee realized she left the door open and absently turned to close it.

"What's the matter, mommy," Jack asked and grabbed a tight hold to Lee's hand.

"Nothing for your pretty little head to worry about," she replied. "Please go finish getting ready for school. And make sure your brother puts on two socks today."

Jack hesitated for just a second before she took off down the hall. In the distance, Lee heard Jack tell her brother it was time for school, then the sound of footsteps as they headed up the stairs to their bedrooms to finish getting dressed.

"I was just served. I'm being sued," Lee said in astonishment, then stared at the envelope like she expected it to come alive and bite her.

Jaxson hobbled over to her, stopping two feet away and careful not to reach for her. He was covered in sweat, and his tee shirt clung to his chest. His breathing was labored, but he was cautious not to rush her.

"Do you have to read it right now? It will still be here when you get home tonight." He fought the urge to pull her into his arms and fix whatever problems she had with everything the Marine Corps taught him. It almost wasn't enough.

Lee nodded absently again and handed him the letter. She brushed passed him as Jack and Dimitri came back with book bags in tow.

"Okay kiddos, let's go." Lee grabbed her purse and laptop bag from the chair, tipping it over with a loud crash. The unexpected noise snapped her out of her confused trance. She looked around, eyes landing on Jaxson who'd stopped at the doorway and gave him a small smile.

"Hurry up, kiddos. I think your mommy is ready to go!" Jaxson exclaimed. He moved forward to shove the kids toward the door to the garage. Jack and Dimitri went out the door and got in Lee's navy-blue sedan. Lee mouthed thank you and followed them out the door.

Jaxson looked at the letter tempted to open it and see who was suing Lee. And, more importantly, why. He knew a handful of ways to open and reseal the letter without her finding out but decided to wait until Lee came home that evening to find out what the situation was. He set the letter on the counter, pulled out his phone, sent his brother a quick text and turned to go back and finish his exercises. His nurse waited in the doorway, smiling.

"I thought I was going to have to smack your hand there for a minute."

They both laughed as they went back in his room and resumed their workout.

Lee came home from the long workday with one sleepy child on her hip and the other one on the verge of a violent meltdown. She'd stopped for fast food in a weak effort to forestall the coming questions, but just the mention of bath time set both kids off. Jack burst into angry tears and Dimitri, always following in his sister's footsteps, whined around his deep yawns.

"Enough," came a stern voice. "Your mother said bath time so march up those stairs right now." Jaxson stood just behind Lee, in a show of solidarity.

Jack wasn't sure how to react. She was instantly quiet, and so was Dimitri, but her face said that she was quickly calculating her next move. She looked for Dimitri, but he'd already grabbed his favorite stuffed pig from the chair where it waited each day for him to reclaim after school and was heading toward the stairs.

Lee and Jaxson stood, united, and watched Jack realize she wasn't going to win this round. She dropped the food bag that was in her hand and ran upstairs, ostensibly to get ready for her bath.

Jaxson moved to go after her, but Lee stopped him. "It won't be worth the enormous amount of commotion she will make. I'm too tired for this today." She stepped away from Jaxson and took a deep breath. "I should get up there. Dimitri believes that since he can reach the handles, he should be able to shower alone." She said with a tired smile. "Do you need me to cook you something?" she added halting in mid stride. When she bought the food earlier, it had just been for her and the kids. Jaxson had not crossed her mind. And she felt instantly guilty for the oversight of forgetting her house guest.

His smile allayed her fears. "Nope. Maggie made a tuna casserole. It was good enough. You go ahead and deal with the kids. I'll put things away down here."

Lee thanked him with a nod of her head. Her foot had no more than hit the bottom step when the unmistakable sound of fighting drifting down the stairs. Jaxson heard her sigh and slowly ambled back to the kitchen.

Jaxson would never admit it to Lee, but he was ecstatic that his burned skin and broken leg meant that he couldn't climb the stairs to referee the mayhem. He really did feel bad, but he was equally sure he'd cave like a house of cards at the sight of any real tears.

Food put away, he limped his way slowly back to his room. The house was silent, now. Lee must have gotten things under control, he thought. As he got himself settled on the bed and turned on the ball game, volume low, Jaxson wondered if Lee had remembered the letter.

11

After getting both kids bathed, brushed, hydrated, and read to, Lee collapsed on her bed, totally and completely exhausted. The workday had been full of drama and meetings. When she picked the kids up, they too were worse for the wear. She decided to take a shower and rinse the obnoxiousness of the day away. Standing in the soothing warmth of the water, she worried what Jaxson was doing. He had no idea how much she appreciated his support that evening. She was on the verge of losing control herself. *I guess this is why social science says families need two parents,* she thought. Not because one can't do it alone - but it is easier when you have support.

The letter waiting for her down in the kitchen had dominated her thoughts all day. While at work, she'd done an internet search on the law firm. It was a family law practice in California. Seeing that piece of information made her stomach drop. She only knew one person in California that would want to sue her. She laid on the bed and decided tomorrow was soon enough to read the bad news.

Who am I fooling, Lee thought, frustrated with herself. There was no way she could sleep with the question of the mysterious summons running laps through her brain like a racehorse. After what seemed like an eternity of lying in bed alternating between tossing and turning and staring at the ceiling, she gave up. Sleep would remain elusive and there didn't seem to be any relief in sight – except finding out what was in that damned letter. *Ok. Might as well face the fire tonight,* she conceded. Sighing, she sat up and glanced at the door. Well past the time for her to be asleep and fully cognizant of the man sleeping in her dining room downstairs, she put on her bathrobe and slippers before descending the squeaky old wooden stairs. She cringed as the antique wood snapped and popped under her feet. "So much for a quiet creep," she muttered to herself.

The envelope remained unopened on the counter. She reached for it but pulled her hand back quickly. She didn't want to touch it, as if the very envelope itself were poisonous. The painful possibilities had haunted her throughout the workday.

Finally, exhausted and over the anxious stomach that had left her nauseated the entire day, she snatched the letter and ripped it open before her mind could protest what her hand had done. Slowly and deliberately, Lee pulled the thick wad of folded papers from of the envelope. She read the cover letter three times before the words began to make any semblance of sense in her exhausted mind. The pages slipped out of her hand as she covered her growing scream with both her hands. She slid to the floor and there was nothing she could do to stop the tears that ran down her cheeks and left a growing wet spot on her seersucker bathrobe.

She stiffened when a strong muscular arm slid around her neck and pulled her close. Lee found herself face to chest with Jaxson who'd no doubt heard the loud stairs and knew she had finally opened the letter. Unable to fight, Lee gave in to her sobs on Jaxson's chest and cried until there was nothing left.

Slightly embarrassed at the huge tear and snot stain she'd left on Jaxson's t-shirt, she pulled away and hid her face. "I've ruined your shirt," she sniffled.

Jaxson wasn't having it. Using his good hand to turn her face toward him, he gave her a soothing smile. "Don't feel bad. I have other shirts."

Lee gave him slight smile, but that half smile quickly fell into a deep frown of anguish as she her eyes landed on the discarded legal papers on the floor. She slowly picked them up, straightening them and then refolded them.

"Wanna talk about it," Jaxson gently asked.

Lee thought over the answer, then decided that since the issue involved him as well, she should tell him. She took a deep breath to keep from crying again and said, "Dimitri's grandmother has gotten an injunction stopping my adoption because I'm harboring a bombing suspect."

Jaxson looked completely dumbstruck. "Is she talking about me?" he asked incredulously. He'd been called many things and accused of much more, but this took the cake. "I'm a decorated military officer, for fuck's sake. It's my goddamn job to blow up things!" He said with his voice growing louder in anger.

"Jaxson, please, you'll wake the kids and I just can't handle Jack asking me a bunch of questions right now."

Lee stood up and found the envelope where it had landed a few feet away. She carefully put the letters back and placed it on top of the refrigerator.

"Come on, let's talk in here".

Jaxson followed her into the den. They sat on the sofa and Lee began to explain.

"Do you remember my best friend, Bryn," she began. When he nodded, she continued "Dimitri is her son."

Jaxson nodded in understanding but said nothing. Lee was fighting tears again. He looked away to give her a chance to pull herself together.

"She was murdered by her husband right after Dimitri was born. They'd separated while she was pregnant. He'd grown more and more controlling during Bryn's pregnancy. Finally, he demanded that she put their child up for adoption. He was such a selfish piece of shit and he didn't want her taking care of any one but him. She threw him out that day and changed the locks. One morning, when Dimitri was about 3 months old, he called and asked if he could see the baby. I begged her not to go, but she insisted she would be safe. It never occurred to her that he'd actually hurt her. Or little Dimitri. Dom held Bryn and Dimitri hostage for three days before he shot Bryn and Dimitri and then killed himself."

Lee let the tears flow for the best friend that had been there for her through her own pregnancy. Bryn had been there to help her decorate Jack's nursery and had been there to coach her through labor. Losing Bryn and taking in Dimitri was the second hardest thing Lee had ever experienced and bringing all this back was causing a pain in her chest that wouldn't go away any time soon.

Bryn and Lee had been unlikely friends. Lee was a quiet bookworm from an immigrant family while Bryn had been the bouncy and beautiful head cheerleader from a poor but close-knit family. But a shared love of horror movies and stale popcorn had sealed the deal and they'd been all but inseparable from the tenth grade until Bryn's death three years ago.

"Bryn stipulated that if anything happened to her, Dimitri was to be left in my care when Dom started going nuts. We had the paper's drawn up and everything. He never accepted paternity, and Bryn didn't put him on the birth certificate. Didn't matter." she said with a sad laugh. "As Bryn's husband, he was legally Dimitri's father. And with both of them dead, and her parents unable to care for him, Dimitri came to live with me and Jack. I thank God daily Dimitri only had a flesh wound."

"Where did the bullet hit him?" Jaxson asked.

"Grazed him on the head," Lee explained. "He was only a baby, but to this day he hates sudden noises," she said with a smile. He was her Dimitri and that's the way he'll always be - her Dimitri, a little quiet fighter.

"So, this grandmother is trying to take..." Jaxson let the words fade off his tongue.

"Dom's mother has been fighting to take Dimitri from me from the day his parents died. Her son was a fucking nutcase and she's not much better. If she thinks I'd just turn Bryn's son over to her... well, when hell freezes over." Lee was shaking though Jaxson wasn't sure if it was in anger or fear of losing Dimitri.

"And now she's using me against you? I'm so sorry, Lee." Jaxson looked genuinely remorseful.

Lee patted his knee. "I never would have guessed she would go this route. She's tried all kinds of stupid things to delay the adoption. Today was just awful and adding this to the mix just overwhelmed me. I'll call the lawyer tomorrow. I just hope I don't have to go to California for this shit."

Jaxson's eyebrows shot up to his hairline. "Lee, I had no idea you knew such words," he said in feigned outrage. He failed to dodge the smack she aimed at his chest. But she was smiling and that was his goal. When she exhaled, and relaxed her shoulders, he stopped worrying that she was going to shatter and break into a million pieces.

Lee gave Jaxson an unreadable look and declared, "I need some sleep, or I will be an unbearable she-wolf tomorrow." She stood, her hands fumbling over each other as she fidgeted nervously. She couldn't decide what else to say, so she mumbled a quick 'good night' and skittered off to bed. Then paused at the door.

"What are you doing up at this hour," she asked Jaxson.

Jaxson sputtered. He wasn't prepared for her question and it was obvious he didn't have a ready answer.

Lee came back in the room, the discomfort in her posture replaced by motherly concern.

"Jaxson. Why are you up so late? What's wrong?" She crossed her arms and leveled him with a stern glare.

Jaxson crumpled under the look. "I don't really sleep very well. I... keep dreaming of the blast and of Sullivan."

Lee sat down beside Jaxson and took his hand in hers. "Oh Jaxson, I'm so sorry. Who is Sullivan?"

"Sullivan was my partner on that stupid mission. And we were in the Corps together. He was killed in the blast."

Lee covered her mouth and gasped. "I'm so sorry!"

"Some nights I dream of hearing Sully's voice and others I dream of the building blowing up and being buried alive. It's just easier to stay awake."

"That's not exactly healthy, you know." Lee had been able to sense that something was bothering Jaxson, but she had no idea it was this. "Why didn't you say something?"

"I've done enough time on the shrink's couch to know it's PTSD – post-traumatic stress. I'm dealing with it."

"By not sleeping?"

"By avoiding the trauma." Jaxson refused to meet Lee's disbelieving glare. "Lee, I can't deal with all this at once. My injuries, Jack, you..."

"Hey!"

"I didn't mean it like it sounded, I swear. I just meant that with all the changes, therapy would be more than I could handle. Let me get through the surgeries first. Then I'll deal with everything else."

"I guess I see what you mean. But I worry what the lack of sleep does to your ability to heal. I mean, sleep is when the body does it best work to heal itself."

Jaxson laughed, and Lee swatted at his arm.

"Fine, laugh all you want. Don't think you're allowed to have an exhaustion induced meltdown in this house mister." Lee leaned over and lightly smacked Jaxson's cheek before standing up. "Good night."

Jaxson watched her go without a word. Instead of going to bed he sat in the den replaying the evening in his head. He'd decided that even though she was clearly still very pissed with him, Lee's frozen facade was cracking. He wanted them to be at least be friendly enough to co-parent. He'd been in her house a month and they'd finally gotten into a good rhythm. She was even relaxing her guard around him. He had another skin graft surgery coming up, but before he could do that, he needed to make a few calls to some friends in the government about Dimitri's dear old grandmother. She didn't know who she was messing with. Her ridiculous strategy smelled of desperation. And desperation made people do stupid things. He could understand why she'd want her grandson, but her methods were dubious at best. There more going on here than Lee knew or than she was willing to tell him. He smiled to himself. Finally, he might be able make a real difference for his newly formed family.

12

Lee's chat with her lawyer a few days later appeased her mind somewhat, but she was still plagued by a nervous stomach. Deciding the day was a bust, she packed up her laptop and files, and grabbed her handbag from the bottom drawer of her meticulously organized desk. As she walked out, she scribbled a quick message for her administrative assistant letting him know she'd be working from home for the rest of the day. Walking to her car, she did a mental roster of places she could grab lunch that were along her route. But just as she reached her car, her cell phone rang.

Lee groaned loudly as she fumbled with the bags trying to find the misplaced phone. The unknown number hung up just as she'd answered so she got in her car and decided to get on her way before checking the missed call. Traffic was backed up on the freeway and the onramp was a standstill, so she decided to check the voicemail. It was Jaxson's nurse. Slightly alarmed she called the nurse back right way. The harried woman answered on the first ring. "Ms. Anderson, thank heavens," came the out of breath voice on the other end. But it wasn't Natalie's voice on the other end. It was Maggie, the housekeeper.

"Maggie" Lee asked, perplexed.

"Yes, ma'am?" Maggie replied sounding frightened and on the verge of tears.

Before Lee could ask what was happening, Maggie continued. "It's Mr. Upton. He's come down with a high-grade fever. Nat's on the phone with 911. They are coming to take him to the hospital."

Lee held the phone in stunned silence for two heartbeats before saying, "I'm on my way. Ask the paramedics what hospital they are taking him to if the ambulance leaves before I get there." Lee disconnected the call just after getting the woman's agreement. Next, Lee called the kids daycare center and let them know that Maggie would be by to pick them up early. Lee made a mental note to leave pizza money and give Maggie permission to order the kids a movie On Demand. That might briefly save Maggie from Jack's interrogation, but Lee doubted it.

She arrived home just as the paramedics were wheeling Jaxson down the ramp in front of the house. Lee said a silent prayer of thanks to her scattered brain for forgetting to call the carpenter to come remove the ugly wooden structure.

Jaxson's arms and legs were strapped down to the bed. Lee gave the medics the same stern look she gave her children.

"He was fighting us. We didn't want him to get hurt. The nurse inside suggested it," the man said defensively.

Lee merely frowned and stepped over to the bed. "Jaxson, why on Earth are you fighting the EMTs? They are trying to help you." Lee took inventory of Jaxson's face - glassy, cloudy eyes; sweat along the hairline and upper lip; constantly licking of his lips.

"They wouldn't wait for you. I had to tell you something important," Jaxson croaked out. He motioned with his chin for Lee to lean down so he could see her better. His eyes locked on hers as he said, "I've only ever loved you. I ran away when I realized how much I loved you, but it's always been you. Even now that you hate me, I'm still in love with my Lee-Lee." His voice trailed off and his eyes closed leaving Lee stunned in silence. The medics took her silence for the end of the conversation and pushed the lightly snoring Jaxson toward the back of the ambulance.

Natalie came rushing outside with her things. She paused and told Lee, "I'm going to follow the ambulance."

Lee snapped to attention and grabbed Natalie by the arm. "What happened," she asked quickly.

"When I arrived this morning, Jaxson had a low-grade fever. I went to help him remove his compression tee shirt and shorts, so I could check his wounds and he wasn't wearing them. Apparently, he hadn't been for some time. I believe he has an infection on his chest wound." She rolled her eyes and frowned. "I tried to reduce the fever and talked to his doctor, but then his fever spiked, despite my best efforts. He needs antibiotics. I could just strangle him." Natalie pushed her bright red hair away from her face and frowned at Lee. She'd felt so helpless when she was unable to stop the fever and worried that Jaxson would suffer long-term damage. The man was, simply put, infuriating.

"I know exactly what you mean. Go, ahead, I'll meet you there."

"Okay," Natalie replied. "We're heading to Memorial. His doctor will be waiting for us." She took off at a jog to her car. Lee watched as the woman's little black convertible shot down the street in the same direction as the ambulance.

Lee jumped when Maggie laid a hand on her shoulder. "Is there anything I can do?" Maggie asked gently.

Lee smiled as she turned around. Maggie was rapidly becoming a friend. "Yes, please. I've let the school know you'd be by to pick up the kids. Use some of the kitchen petty cash to order a pizza and a movie for the kids. I'll apologize up front for the coming interrogation."

Maggie's bright laugh lightened Lee's mood. "I've been subjected to Jack's rapid-fire questioning more than once; I'll be the first to admit it makes me appreciate my slightly less brilliant child even more." Both women laughed, taking advantage of the brief break in the drama. "Do you want me to bring the kids to the hospital later, today?"

Lee gave the question some thought but shook her head. "No, thanks. I'll go and check on Jaxson and will try to be back by your normal leave time. I'll be sure to call if I'll be late, but I'm going to call Jaxson's dad and brother, so they can deal with his stubborn butt." She shook her head once more and turned to her car.

Maggie's voice stopped her in her tracks. "One other thing, Lee. As his fever went up and he became more delirious, all he could talk about was how he was a coward for leaving you. And how much he loved you. He was fighting the EMT's because he knew Nat had called you and he didn't want to leave until you got home. He's really strong, you know?" Maggie smiled. "Despite the 103-degree fever he could wrestle two fully trained EMTs. I know he was a Marine, but I thought he was just a scientist."

Lee smiled at that, though she was still fairly stunned by his admission.

"You better go. I'll get, Jack and Dimitri, and everything will be okay here," Maggie said absolving Lee from formulating a response. They exchanged a wordless look before Lee rushed to her car, jumped in and pulled off.

During the ten-minute ride to the hospital, Lee made contact with Lukas. She gave him a brief rundown of what she knew, including the fact that he'd stopped wearing the compression clothing as instructed. "I can wait at the hospital for news until six then I have to go relieve Maggie."

Lukas agreed to call Pop and promised they'd be at the hospital as soon as possible. Disconnecting from the call, Lee's mind turned to Jaxson's fever induced confession. She didn't know what to make of it. More than that, she couldn't figure out how she felt about it. Lee didn't hate Jaxson. Far from it. But neither did she trust him. In all honesty, she had every expectation that he'd go back to his life at first chance and leave her behind again. *Maybe things really were different this time*, she thought. Before she could fall too far into that rabbit hole, her phone rang again - this time it was her lawyer.

"Hello Dan," she said connecting to the cell through a button on her steering wheel.

"Lee," he responded with a booming voice, loud and clear through the car's speakers. A Texas native, Dan's thick country accent made Lee's name sound like a two-syllable word. "Bad news, the judge let the injunction stand, though we did get Wilhelmina's case moved to Charlotte."

Lee was heartbroken. They were two weeks from the final adoption. "I see," was all she could say without falling apart.

"Don't fret. We'll get this straightened out. Those touchy freely California judges don't have an ounce of sense." He paused, and Lee's stomach fell. The blood rushed to her ears and she almost missed his follow up question. "How well do you know your new roommate?"

"He's Jacinta's biological father. He's a US Marine Corps officer." Lee's hackles were raised. *Why is that important,* she thought angrily. *And why is this any of that crazy old bat's business?*

"Okay. Just be aware, it's likely he will be subpoenaed by Wilhelmina's lawyers. I'd like the chance to talk to him before the hearing."

"He was just taken to the emergency room with an infection and fever. I'm on my way there now," Lee cried. She couldn't hold back the tears any longer. "I don't know when he will be able to talk to anyone." She took several deep breaths as she pulled into a parking space. Lee sent up a prayer for strength.

"I'll put in for a continuance. I'm sure he'll be fine, Lee," Dan replied trying to console his client. "We'll get all this worked out. I promise."

"Thanks, Dan. I've just pulled up to the hospital. I'll give you a call tomorrow and we'll be able talk at length." She paused, then asked, "Did Wilhelmina ask for something? Why is she doing this?"

Dan's sigh rang through the speakers. "She's saying that you're an unfit parent and that her family should rightfully have custody of Dmitri and Jack."

Lee was stunned. "What do you mean custody of Jack? Jack isn't her blood."

"They've filed a complaint in family court to have both kids removed from your care. I've put in a motion to have that abandoned, but they'll bring it up in court. If you want my professional opinion, her plan is to harass you into giving the boy up."

"Her son murdered Bryn and tried to kill Dmitri. That is never going to happen!" Lee yelled and took a breath then sighed. "I'm sorry, Dan. I didn't mean to yell."

"Lee, we're working to get this thrown out. The change in venue may help. One last thing. Would you be willing to offer non-supervised visitation?"

Lee thought that over. Her mind wasn't in the right place to give it rational thought. "I don't know," she said honestly. "Let's talk about this tomorrow."

Dan agreed and reiterated his point that this would be worked out and the adoption would be finalized before disconnecting the call. Lee's faith was beginning to waiver. Pushing that thought aside, Lee grabbed her purse and headed to ER.

Easily enough, she found Natalie watching a soap opera on the television in the waiting room.

"Nat!" Lee called out. Lee walked over and sat next to the nurse. "How is he?"

Natalie ran a tired hand through her pixie cut naturally red hair. "Just as I thought, it's an

LORI A. HENDRICKS

infection. Apparently, he's been feeling the effects of it for some time, judging how widespread the infection is. Stupid man never said a word."

Lee put a hand on Nat's leg. "Well, hopefully he hasn't done any permanent damage to himself."

"The last graft they did on his upper arm will have to be removed and the graft scheduled for his chest will have to be postponed," Natalie added quickly. Jaxson was going to be big pain in all of their asses after hearing this news.

Lee fell back in the chair. The broken bones were healing, but he burned much of his forearm and the mobility of the elbow joint depended on the success of the skin grafts. Jaxson was going to be livid, but he had no one to blame but himself. *Stubborn jackass*, Lee thought.

"Perhaps, now, he'll follow his healing regiment," Lee said, but both women knew that was highly unlikely. Jaxson had always thought he knew better than everyone else, no matter the subject. And beyond that he had such high and rigorous expectations of himself that he accepted very little human weakness. Lee was not looking forward to any conversation about him taking things more slowly and following a strict rehabilitation plan.

"He's asleep and they're trying to reduce the fever." Nat blushed and added with a sheepish grin.

• 112 •

"I, uh, told them you were his wife, so they'd give you the updates."

Lee rolled her eyes and as if on cue, a tall buffalo of a man in the biggest white coat Lee was sure she'd ever seen walked in, stopping just in front of Lee and Natalie.

"Mrs. Chase? I'm Dr. Bryant."

Lee and Natalie stood up, and Lee swallowed past the lump in her throat to reply, "How are you, doctor?"

"I'm well, thank-you. And so," He transitioned with a big smile, "is your husband, despite clearly pushing himself entirely too hard, and not following the requirement to wear his compression garments at all times. He is responding well to the treatment. He still has a fever, but he is out of danger."

"Oh, thank goodness!" Nat exclaimed elbowing Lee as subtly as she could manage.

"Yes, fantastic. Is he ... my husband awake?" Lee hoped her voice sounded steady, because she most certainly didn't feel it.

"No, Mrs. Chase. Your husband is sleeping, but we expect he will wake soon." The doctors deep voice echoed across the empty room.

"Oh good," Lee exclaimed with what she hoped was the right amount of vigor. Honestly, she wanted to get home to the kids. She was unaccountably uncomfortable pretending to be

Jaxson's wife. "I will be here until Jaxson's father and brother arrive, then I'll be getting back to the kids. I left them with a friend," she added quickly.

The doctor nodded, still somewhat unsure what he was missing but sure that he had, in fact, missed something. "Natalie can show you to his bed, so I'll leave you to it." He walked away, his long legs and brisk pace carried him away from the area with an unbelievable quickness.

Nat gave Lee a sincerely annoyed look. "Remind me never to take you on a covert mission." The frown was quickly replaced by a wide smile and she led Lee to Jaxson's room.

13

Jaxson was awake and more or less alert when Lee stepped through the curtain. *Of course he's up*, she thought somewhat uncharitably. "You are supposed to the sleep," she said, her voice harder than she'd wanted.

He winced. "Are you going to lecture me too," he whispered peering at her over the covers with one eye open and the other squeezed tightly shut.

"No," she replied adding with a smug amount of sugar to her voice, "but I am going to tell Jack exactly how you ended up here." The smile she gave him wasn't friendly.

"Lee," Jaxson warned, opening both eyes wide with fear. It was ridiculous that a Marine whose job is to bomb and de-bomb buildings in war torn countries would be scared to face one small girl, but Jack's interrogations were merciless. "Lee, I swear I'll do better. Don't sic Jack on me. You know how she is about rules."

Jaxson learned the hard way that his daughter was a stickler about rules and order. She had memorized his schedule and any deviation caused a ten-minute stream of questioning. And she never once accepted 'I don't know' as a valid answer.

He could see that he wasn't going to get any sympathy from Lee. And he really shouldn't. He thought he was healing and didn't need the compression garments. How was he to know they kept the skin protected from injury and germs, he thought sourly. Now he was back in the hospital, tubes and needles flowing every which way. He deserved the abuse for putting Lee and the kids through this, not to mention Natalie and Maggie.

As Lee turned to leave and let him rest, Jaxson yelped. "Hey, wait...How did you get them to let you back here?"

Lee blushed and some of the smug dropped from her smile. "Well - Natalie told them I was your estranged wife. Your continued declarations of eternal and never-ending love and repeated vows of contrition convinced both the paramedics and triage nurses." She couldn't quite keep eye contact. "So, I went with it. I knew they wouldn't tell me anything, if I didn't. And you know Jack has to know all the details."

Jaxson couldn't tell what bothered Lee more - him telling her he loved her in his fevered state or Lee having to pretend to be his wife. Probably both, he decided to let out a ragged sigh and an, "I see".

"Do you need anything? Your dad and Lukas should be here soon, and I need to get home. Maggie picked up the kids and I still have work to get done before I go to the office tomorrow. You don't seem to be dying, and I need to tell Jack the good news before she drives Maggie to quit. I really like her, you know."

"Lee," he started but the shake of her head cut off that line of thought. He accepted it. They would discuss it another time. "I'm fine. I should probably get some sleep before Pop gets here to rip me a new one."

Lee laughed though the smile didn't reach her eyes. Jaxson felt bad for causing her more pain. He didn't try to stop her when she turned to go but released a held breath when she turned back.

She reached in her pocket and pulled out his cell phone. "Nat gave me this to give to you." She pulled a charger out of her purse and plugged it in, wrapping the plug around the side table, so it didn't fall. "Just in case. If you get a chance, call Jack, and let her know you are okay. You know how she worries."

He thanked her, and they exchanged awkward goodbyes before she left the room.

By the time Lukas and Pop arrived, Jaxson's fever had broken, and he was feeling better, but still rather weak.

As expected, Pop launched into a loud and excessively profane lecture immediately. "You are a stubborn jackass, and you should be ashamed of yourself for ending up here." His voice was just shy of a full bellow. Lukas laid a hand on the old man's arm, hoping to calm him down some. Jaxson and Pop fought like crazy, but no one could argue that father and son were not absolutely devoted to one another. Jaxson's sickness was too much too soon on the heels of the explosion.

"Pop," Lukas said softly. "Calm down or you'll end up in the bed next to Jaxson. He's fine. Lee told us."

Jaxson eyes perked open. "You talked to Lee? What did she say? She still planning to tell Jack about this?" He grabbed the remote and used the controller to raise the head of the bed and prop himself up. The process was slow, and the frustration was written all over Jaxson's creased forehead.

Lukas fought a laugh. "She said she had just left here, you were slightly delirious, but would be okay." Jaxson started to relax, them Lukas added, "She also said you were here because you weren't following the regiment that the doctors laid out. She also said you'd managed to undo your last surgery and now they're postponing your next surgery. I'd say it's a good bet that she's still going to tell Jack that you're an idiot. And you deserve no less."

Pop's eyes nearly bugged out of his head. Jaxson merely mumbled "Snitch," and turned his head toward the wall. Lukas grabbed Pop, who was about to hit Jaxson upside the head and turned him toward the door.

"Go visit your friend and calm down. I'll talk to Jaxson and make sure he understands how important this rehabilitation is. Okay?"

Pop grabbed the hat that had fallen to the floor and wandered out the room mumbling "stubborn horse's ass" under his breath. Lukas and Jaxson waited until Pop was well away before Lukas turned back to his younger brother and asked, "Lesson learned?"

Jaxson smiled and replied "Yep. Lee's going to tell Jack what I've done to myself. I mean... I don't think that's necessary, do you?" He couldn't help the hint of whine in his voice. He loved Jack without question, but good grief she was tenacious. She'd definitely have a future in the CIA or FBI. Easily.

Lukas blanched. He too had been on the receiving end of one of Jack's interrogations and he thanked God every time he saw his new niece that Ava couldn't talk that well yet. He made a mental note to limit Ava's exposure to her inquisitive cousin as she got older. "I'm sorry to hear that, but yes. This cannot happen again. She's the best deterrent ever created."

They shared a laugh as Lukas brought a chair closer to Jaxson. He lowered his voice and added, "I have some info on that person you asked me to look into."

For the next thirty minutes, Lukas relayed all the information gathered on Dimitri's family. His grandmother was the wealthy matriarch of a family of Greek wine growers in California. Dom had been the spoiled younger son who'd married Bryn against the family's wishes.

"Wilhelmina insists that Bryn killed Dom then committed suicide despite all evidence to the contrary. She sued the city and Charlotte police department when the final report saying the contrary was released to the media."

Jaxson chewed on this bit of information. It would seem that filing suit against Lee was par for the old woman's course, he thought. "She sounds like a real piece of work," was what he said aloud.

Lukas looked thoughtful. "There is more, but I don't know if you want to hear it though."

"I'm no schoolgirl, Lukas." Jaxson said jokingly. "You aren't going to shock me."

Lukas laughed softly. "Um, Jack is a schoolgirl and is kinda scary with that big brain of hers."

Jaxson nodded in agreement. "I need to know what Lee is going through, but Lee won't tell me." He left it at that. He could tell something other than his fever and infection was on her mind today, but she opted not to confide in him - not that he could blame her.

"Lee is nearly broke. The house, the kids and Wilhelmina's constant lawsuits are bleeding her dry. I'm sure the old woman knows it. Lee may have the law on her side, but financially she won't be able to keep up the fight for much longer"

Jaxson groaned and flopped back on the bed. "And this last lawsuit is because she took me in. Shit."

Lukas nodded. "Wilhelmina has some eyewitnesses that have sworn that you are responsible for the bombing downtown and that the government is covering it up because you're a war hero."

Jaxson couldn't speak for long while. "Does Lee know this," he asked, his rage barely contained. He'd never wanted to hit an old woman in his life, but if he ever got the chance, he'd clean Wilhelmina's clock.

"I don't know," Lukas replied. "I do know you are on the subpoena list, but since you're back in the hospital, the hearing and your deposition will most likely get pushed back."

Jaxson absently shook his head in weak denial. "She didn't say anything."

"I'm sure her lawyer - who is worth every penny of his exorbitant fee - is working to get all this thrown out. He got the case moved from San Francisco to Charlotte since that's where everything happened. The old lady is furious about that." Lukas grinned in admiration. The file he'd read on Wilhelmina Andris painted the picture of a privileged woman with no qualms about using her name and wealth to get what she wanted. Dom had been her only son, meaning Dimitri was her only chance to carry on the family name. The private investigator he'd hired could find no evidence the woman cared at all about her grandson - merely the continuation of the Andris Wine dynasty.

"So, what do we do," Lukas asked. "I don't think Lee will thank me for prying into her personal business and she'll certainly never let me help pay for this. She only accepted Maggie because she really needed the help."

Lee was an amazing mom, but she only had two hands. Keeping up with Jack would be enough for anyone, but throw in Dimitri and everything else, and it had become clear to Jaxson that the woman was on the verge of cracking. This latest round with Wilhelmina might actually push her over the edge of insanity.

Jaxson then wondered how his current situation contributed to her stress levels. The two were finally rebuilding their friendship. She may not love him as she once had, but she no longer shied away as she had when she first visited him in the hospital. He felt even more guilt. "I don't know, Luke. Should I move out? I can go live with Pop." Just the thought made his blood pound in his ears.

"The train has already left that station, little brother. Moving out will only make you look guilty. I do think we need to get you a lawyer." He pulled a card out and handed it to Jaxson. "Don't argue. I've already got one on retainer. They are waiting for your call."

Jaxson surprised his brother by not only not arguing, but by thanking him for everything he'd done. Jaxson laughed at the stricken look on his brother's face. "I'm way out of my league with this one, big brother. I'll take all the help I can get. Besides, what's the point of having a rich relative if you can't spend their money?"

14

Lee arrived home and relieved a visibly frustrated Maggie. "She's full of questions," she warned as she grabbed her purse and jacket, nearly running out the door. Lee sighed as she locked the door behind the housekeeper and walked to the den. The kids had set up a pallet on the floor, having laid the cushions from the sofa down and each brought their comforters and pillows from their bedrooms. Lee watched them from the doorway as they laughed at the silly cartoon dogs on the television screen. She slipped off her shoes and tip toed in, dropping down between them. Dimitri crawled on her lap and Jack snuggled up to her mom's side, pulling Lee's arm around her shoulders. Lee sighed in utter contentment, yet she couldn't help but think Jaxson should be there with them.

Jack caught her mom's frown. "Don't worry mommy, I'm not going to ask a bunch of questions. Miss Maggie said you were stressed out because daddy made himself sick. But can I ask one question?"

Lee looked down at Jack's sad eyes and tried to smile reassuringly. "You may ask as many questions as you need to," she gave Jack's shoulder a strong, tight squeeze.

"Is daddy going to die?" Jack asked sounding every bit the little four-year-old girl she was. Her enhanced intellect made it easy to forget just how young she really was at times.

Lee sat up and made sure both kids could see her face. "I talked to your dad and he's going to be fine. And Maggie was right. He didn't follow the doctor's orders and that's why he got sick. I'm sure he's learned his lesson and won't let it happen again. Jack, I know he'd be really happy to have you help him stay on schedule. We can make a big one for him when he gets home. We can ask Miss Natalie to help, too."

Jack's face brightened up at the thought. "We're gonna need more construction paper."

Lee laughed as Jack named all the things they would need for this grand schedule she wanted to make. Lee made a solemn oath to take them to the craft store and then agreed to watch one video with them before going to get some work done.

Dimitri picked the next show and Lee said a silent prayer thanking whoever was responsible for creating on-demand programming. The cartoon was genuinely hilarious. Lee often wondered when watching some of these kids shows just how many of the jokes the kids really got. She didn't want to ask, not really, preferring to think of her babies as just that - babies - and innocent as can be for as long as she's able.

At the end of the show, she loathed the idea of leaving the kids, but knew she had to get to work but decided returning calls could wait until tomorrow. She ran upstairs and changed into comfy sweats, pulled her hair up into a loose bun before going back downstairs. Then she grabbed her files along with her laptop and rejoined the kids in the living room, much to the kids delight. The house phone rang from the kitchen and Lee let Jack answer. From Jack's rapid-fire questioning, Lee figured she'd guessed correctly, and it was Jaxson that had called.

Thirty email replies and four episodes later, everyone was yawning, Lee included. She first carried Dimitri upstairs, stripped his clothes, and put on his pajamas. She felt a moment of guilt for not making him brush his teeth, and she made a silent vow to herself to make sure he brushed them twice as long in the morning. It wasn't long before the sleeping boy was all tucked in with the spare blanket from the sofa.

She turned to go down for Jack, but there Jack stood with one ponytail askew and rubbing her eyes. Lee smiled and took Jack by the shoulders, turned her around and led her to her bedroom. Lee sat on the bed while the little girl changed into her pajamas, then brushed her teeth. She climbed into bed and Lee tucked her in, snug as a bug in a rug.

"Want a story tonight?" Lee asked, holding the chapter book they'd been slowly working their way through.

Jack yawned before replying, "Not tonight, mommy," She paused then asked, "How long will daddy be gone?"

"I don't know. He had a high fever and an infection, so they have to fix that before they will let him come... home." Lee paused slightly as the word got stuck in her throat.

Jack giggled. "Ok mommy", she yawned wide and snuggled down in her bed. "Night, night mommy!" she said half asleep already.

"Night, baby girl," She turned off the light and pulled the door almost to closed, leaving it just open enough to let a sliver of light into the girl's room.

Lee grabbed her cell phone and ran down the steps to the den. As she undertook cleaning up the makeshift beds to kids had left on the floor, her phone buzzed, letting her know she had a text message.

"You up?" from Jaxson.

"Yes," she replied.

"Can we talk about what I said earlier?" came his response, quickly.

Lee read and re-read the message. She clicked the screen off and set the phone down. She picked up a blanket and began to fold it. Her phone rang twice in rapid succession.

"Lee?" the first message said. "I meant everything I said today." came the second. Lee stared at the screen. Absently she lowered herself to the sofa.

Lee had no idea what she felt or how to respond. In fact, she'd purposefully avoided thinking about Jaxson's earlier declaration of love. Another ding, another message. "Good night", it said.

"Jaxson," Lee typed into her phone. "I don't know what I feel anymore." She added.

"I understand," he replied.

"I don't think you do, I sure don't," she sent. Then thought about how to say what was truly in her heart. She started and erased the message many times before finally sending, "I need more time."

Jaxson's response of, "Ok" ended the conversation.

Lee placed the phone down and immediately busied herself with cleaning the room. *Easy enough,* she thought. She mindlessly moved around the room, setting things back where they belonged. She thought about Jaxson's brief time with her little family. He truly belonged. Quite easily he'd become a comfortable presence, providing a balance that had been missing in all their lives.

She couldn't deny the effect Jaxson had on Dimitri. He'd healed from his physical wounds, but he wasn't the happy-go-lucky baby he was before the attack. Jaxson was bringing the boy out of his shell in a way Lee had not been able to. He'd had a similar effect on Jack. She'd always been a very serious child, who didn't seem to relate to other kids - neither the ones her age nor the other kids in her gifted classes. Jaxson helped her be comfortable in her own skin and she was socializing better. Jack had come home the week before with her first birthday party invitation from a kid her own age. She was over the moon and insisted that she was going to be popular. Lee couldn't deny the correlation between Jaxson's arrival and the fact that both kids were happier.

But as much as she could appreciate Jaxson's relationship with the kids, that didn't mean he was ready to be with her. Or did it? Jaxson had never expressed any desire for a family. He seemed like a totally different person, but Lee couldn't bring herself to trust it. She had to protect herself and the kids, or so she thought. She wasn't going to let her heart override her brain. She'd let that happen once, and that's how life ended up crashing into her lap. She needed a plan – something she could rely on and cling to. Something logical and sound. She loved her kids with all her heart, but Jaxson? He was a totally different story. Or so she told herself as she dragged herself up the stairs to bed.

15

After a couple days in the hospital, Jaxson was finally allowed to go home – that's how he had begun to think of the old wooden Victorian house with Lee, Dimitri, and Jack. It was one of the happiest returns he had, even taking into account each of his deployments. And despite the fancy new schedule affixed to the wall next to his television, he was instantly relaxed and at ease. Until, that is, Jack and Dimitri came home from school. Jack walked in slowly, setting her bag on the chair as evidence of the day's trip to the library fell across the floor. Jaxson was in his room rocking in the recliner next to the window, an old ugly chair of pops that Jaxson had demanded be brought over. He had just enough time to pull himself up right before Dimitri bolted into the room, launching himself into Jaxson's still tender arms.

"I'm okay, I promise." Jaxson grunted out. He was reassuring a fretting and distressed Dimitri, but his eyes never left Jack's calculating eyes. "Jack, can I have a hug?" he asked. He could tell she was still working through her feelings.

"Jack, you may ask me anything you want, no matter how long it takes." Jaxson hoped he wouldn't regret those words as Lee walked in.

Having heard what he'd said she raised her eyebrows and shrugged, deciding to let Jaxson be the master of his own destiny. Instead of saving him from an evening of interrogation and fussing, she laughed.

Eyes back on Jack, Jaxson patiently waited, but she merely nodded.

"Do I have you to thank for the schedule," he asked pulling Dimitri up onto his lap and taking the pressure off the burns on his arms.

Jack's face perked up. She bounced over to the wildly decorated poster board, beaming. There were stickers from at least five superheroes, a wide variety of jungle cats and enough glitter that it left a sizable pile on the floor.

"Miss Natalie told me and mommy what you have to do to get better and not get sick again. Mommy helped me with the days, and she had to write the activities. Then me and Dimitri decorated it. Do you like it?"

"You know it. Now, I'll never forget anything ever again." Jaxson smiled wide and hoped Jack missed the slight of tinge sarcasm in his voice.

"Right. And you won't die. And Miss Natalie said I could come by in the morning and remind you of your schedule. Especially on the weekends when she's not here. She said I could be your nurse. Isn't that the best, daddy?" Jack gave her mother, then, her father a big smile. She spent hours memorizing Jaxson schedule so she could help.

"Okay, you two grab your books and put them in your room. Decide what book we're going to read at bedtime, then get ready for dinner."

Dimitri seemed hesitant to let Jaxson go, but finally he jumped down and ran forward to take Jack's hand. The two took off running for their bedrooms and Jaxson waited until the pounding of the kids' feet on the rickety wooden stairs indicated they were, for the moment out of earshot.

Lee walked to the bed and sat on the corner closest to Jaxson. She focused her eyes on picking lint off the bedspread and asked, "Are you planning to stay?"

Jaxson was taken aback. "Yes, I'm staying. Unless you were planning to put me out," he asked with a laugh that dropped when he saw the look on her face.

"I seriously thought about it. But it's not your fault having you so close is making my brain short out." Lee went back to picking at the invisible lint as Jaxson tried to process her words.

"Lee, baby, I'm so sorry. I never intended to make things harder for you. Just tell me how you want to proceed, and I'll do it." He prayed for her to look at him, so he'd be able to look in her eyes. Lee's emotions were always so easily read in her eyes. She knew it, and so she refused to look at him. Jaxson's face fell. He felt lost and confused, and so he sat back and waited for her to say something.

"Just give me time," she said "I don't know what to think and I don't know what to do. And I'm not ready to dive down that rabbit hole right with you now. The situation with Dimitri is my primary focus."

Jaxson peeked around to make sure the kids hadn't somehow made it down the stairs without them knowing it. "About that," he started. He leaned forward before continuing. "When you told me about that lawsuit and that I was the reason for this latest round of drama, I had Lukas hire someone to look into the lawsuit and Dimitri's grandmother."

He paused for a moment to let her digest this new information. She didn't look angry, so he started talking again. "Lukas made a bunch of money when he and his business partner sold their last two startups. I could kick myself for not investing." Jaxson smile, but Lee's confused face spurred him to continue the tale. "Anyway, I wanted to know what you were going to be up against and what I could to do to protect you and the kids."

"Mom!" Jack's shrill voice was followed by a loud crash and a scream.

Lee jumped up and ran out the door, through the kitchen to the stairs, Jaxson close behind. She took the stairs two at a time as the unmistakable sound of glass breaking reached them. Jack and Dimitri were on the top bunk of Jack's bed. On the floor was a large rock and broken glass.

Lee ran over to the kids and checked them for injury. Jaxson went straight to the window, but whomever had been out there was now gone. "What happened?" Lee couldn't let the kids go. She was trembling.

"Someone was on the roof outside Dimitri's room, so we ran in here. Then he threw the rock and I made Dimitri get on my bed and hide. I was

scared so I called you. I was so scared mommy."
Jack's bottom lip was trembling, and it didn't take
much for the little girl to start to cry.

Lee pulled Jack off the bed and cradled the child
in her arms as she fell apart. Jack hung on to Lee's
neck for dear life. Unable to manage the additional
weight, Lee slid to the floor with Jack crying wildly,
like the frightened child she was. Jaxson plucked
Dimitri off the bunk and carried him out the room
to give Lee and Jack a chance to settle down.

Lee held on to Jack and pushed down the lump
of fear she felt. This was Jack's room, but she
couldn't help but feel that Dimitri was most likely
the target. She couldn't believe Wilhelmina would
go this far, but Lee couldn't deny that people in
that family had old world ties and believed
wholeheartedly in the theory of 'by any means
necessary' to get what they wanted.

She reflected on what she knew and remembered
what Jaxson was trying to tell her. She needed to
find out more about what the investigator
discovered. Jack's sobs finally slowed down. Lee
pulled away and looked at her daughter. "Are you
okay, baby," she asked, wiping Jack's flushed
cheeks, and giving the girl a reassuring smile. "You
were brave, very brave, to try to save your brother.
I'm very proud of you."

"Was he going to take Dimitri? "Jack asked, the wheels of her mind turning furiously.

"I don't know, sweetie," Lee answered honestly and settled in because Jack was gearing up for a long interrogation.

"Is this because his grandma wants him to come live with her?" Jack's eyes were just like her mother's – they showed every twist, turn, and pivot of her emotions.

Lee shouldn't have been surprised that Jack knew what was going on. Jack had long since mastered the art of absorbing every drop of information around her. She sighed and she realized her careful tiptoeing around the subject had failed spectacularly.

"If this really was about Dimitri, then yes that is an option. Dimitri's grandmother is trying to bring him to live with her, but when Dimitri's mom and dad died, they wanted him to live with me. So, there has been some legal stuff to decide where Dimitri should live." Lee paused to see if Jack understood what she said.

"I don't want Dimitri to go, mommy." Jack declared with a definite nod. "Does daddy have to move for us to keep Dmitri? You and daddy aren't married yet!" She looked up at her mom, eyes wide with fear.

"Jack, please don't worry. Your dad and Dimitri aren't going anywhere anytime soon." Lee hugged the child wondering if she believed what she was saying.

"What about when daddy is all better? Will he leave then?" And it was obvious that Jack had been worrying about this for a quite some time. Lee felt bad that she'd been so preoccupied with Jaxson and the lawsuits that she hadn't noticed her baby girl had been suffering from all these anxieties. She gave her daughter another tight squeeze.

"I don't know what will happen. No one does, Jack. But I can say this – you're absolutely right that your dad and I aren't married, and he might move out when he can take care of himself. But he will never leave you and Dimitri. He has fallen very much in love with both of you and he'd rather cut off his good leg before losing you two."

"And you too mommy?" Jack scrambled out of her mother's arms and gave her a thorough look.

Lee's face flushed. She gave a pained sigh to stall for time as she figured out how to respond. "That's enough questions for now." She forced a smile. Luckily Jack ran out the room in search of her dad and brother. Lee busied herself with picking up broken bits of glass, then toys and clothes and so she didn't hear Jaxson come in the room.

"I missed you," he said softly. "More than you realize." He waited a moment before taking another step into the room. "I missed you when I deployed that first time and damn near every day since. Even though I know it couldn't ever happen, whenever we'd come back from a tour, I always searched the waiting crowd for you. I just wished somehow you'd know how much I needed you." He reached a hand out and brushed her hair out of her face, his knuckles lightly brushed her cheek.

Lee stared at her hands and let his words wash over and through her. She looked up at him and gave him a confused smile. She took a step back and whispered, "after the kids go to bed, we'll talk." She frowned, thought for a second, them said, "Wait – how did you make it upstairs?"

"The kids were in danger. I didn't think about it. But I couldn't get back down. Dimitri wanted some water, but I can't bend my leg enough to walk down the stairs." He blushed and ducked his head in embarrassment

"Oh. Well, okay." She stood up and walked over to him and smiled. "I know that made you sick to say out loud."

"Lee, do you think Wilhelmina is responsible for this?" Jaxson walked past Lee with a sheet and the staple gun from the storage closet down the hall.

Lee followed him to the window with a pensive look on her face. "I do. And I'm not sure what to do about it." She held the sheet up for Jaxson to staple. They moved to the other side of the window before he responded.

"I think first we should file a police report, so we have a record of it. If this harassment continues or gets worse, we want the cops to know."

They finished covering Jack's window with a sheet off the bed in silence. Jaxson straightened up from adding a few extra staples to the bottom of the window and found himself face to face to Lee.

"Can the kids go to bed, now?" He asked flashing a bright smile

Lee blushed. "We should probably feed them first," she said laughing.

"Kids, time for dinner." Jaxson yelled over his shoulder as Lee wrapped an arm around his lower back and he wrapped his good arm around her shoulder. Jack and Dimitri ran past them down the stairs at top speed. Laughing, and moving as carefully as they could, Lee and Jaxson made their way down to the kitchen for dinner.

The police came and took statements from everyone but Dimitri who held on to Jaxson so tight he was sure to have bruises on his arm. Dimitri was so shaken up that he'd gone back to chewing on his fingers and biting his lip. Lee was beside herself. Jack wasn't much better. She recounted her story but burst into tears when the policeman asked her to describe the man that threw the rock. Jaxson made sure to get a copy of the report and the officer's card before escorting them out.

After a subdued dinner of pizza and juice, both kids were ready for bed. It took less than 20 minutes for them to be properly tucked in, books read, teeth brushed, and forehands kissed. Exhausted herself, Lee finally made her way into the den. Jaxson grabbed the remote and turned the TV off to give Lee his undivided attention. She sat next to him and folded her arms in her lap.

Jaxson waited patiently for Lee to gather her thoughts. Earlier in the evening he'd decided to let her take the lead and stay quiet. But he should have known that strategy wouldn't last.

"Lee, I know I'm putting you in a weird position, and I'll go if that makes you feel better," he declared, his words rushed and jumbled. It was clear that leaving was the last thing Jaxson wanted.

Lee wondered how to respond. She didn't want Jaxson to leave either. The realization struck her deep in her gut. When they were together the first time, she'd tried to hold herself aloof to protect her heart. And though she and Jaxson hadn't been together long, his carefree manner and bright smile made him easy to love. He'd wormed his way into her heart quickly, so his abandonment (which is how she had always thought of his actions) would make the pain that much worse. No woman wants to know that the man she loved didn't love her and she was no exception.

But she couldn't deny how much more relaxed she'd been since Jaxson moved in. The kids were happier and having someone else in the house for the two to focus on for stretches of time gave Lee the freedom to take care of projects around the house that she'd never had the time to work on. Lee adored Jack and Dimitri, but she really had to admit to herself that they wore her out sometimes. She considered herself very lucky. Her kids were good and generally well mannered. But both were curious almost to a fault. Just keeping up with near constant barrage of questions kept Lee on her toes all the time.

Jaxson had to have an endless supply of patience, answering the children's questions, and looking up answers without seeming to tire. Perhaps it was their kindred spirits – that made her a bit jealous of the ease that lie between the three.

They truly enjoyed each other's company, whether engrossed in a show or a book or a conversation. But then Jaxson could still look at her in a way that caused her belly to flip and she'd forget she was keeping him at arm's length.

He was watching her that way right now. Moisture pooled between her legs and she fought to maintain some semblance control.

"I don't want you to go. The kids love having you around. Jack is so worried about you going away. You may want to talk to her about that," she added as an afterthought. She was fidgeting and nervous, but more than that, she was also very turned on by having him alone and so close she could smell is soap.

Jaxson had been her last lover. She'd been so heartbroken that she hadn't given any thought to dating. Having Jack, then taking in Dimitri meant that she didn't have time to dwell on the loneliness she felt on those rare occasions that it was quiet, and her mind could stray. It had become normal practice for her to push those feelings as down deep as she could to maintain that sliver of mental health.

Lee's mouth went dry. Jaxson's eyes are glazed over, and it was obvious he too was turned on. Lee licked her lips, as nervousness and arousal battled for control of her body. Her hands gripped each other, and the brown skin of her knuckles went ashen from the force. She tried to smile, tried to think, and formulate words.

She thought for sure her heart stopped beating when Jaxson reached over and place a cautious hand on her cheek. He hesitated, giving her time to react. When she didn't pull away Jaxson slid his hand forward curling her hair through his fingers and around her neck. Giving Lee time to tell him 'no', 'stop', or to push them away, he paused. His intense brown eyes locked with hers. Instead of pushing him away she leaned forward, her lips pressing timidly against his and her arms shaking gracelessly as they slipped around his neck. She pulled him forward, using her weight and gravity to bring Jaxson down on top of her.

Jaxson wasn't sure how to proceed. Lee was kissing him. Of that there was no doubt, but Jaxson couldn't help but wonder why. Lee must have felt his confusion. She pulled away, head cocked slightly to the side, her brow furrowed in embarrassment and confusion.

"I'm sorry," she started, but Jaxson kissed her softly, quieting her apology.

Pulling himself up onto his elbows, he said, "No, I just want you to be sure this is what you want, because as much as I want you right now, I refuse to do anything to hurt you again."

Lee took in Jaxson's words and instantly bristled in anger. She put her hands on his chest and pushed, but in her position, she couldn't muster up much strength.

Jaxson reared back, "What? What did I say?"

"Damn it, Jaxson! Why do you always think you know better than I do about what I want or don't want or what I can or can't handle?" Lee squeezed out from under Jaxson before he could stop her. Breathing raggedly, Lee paced in a tight circle.

"Lee... Lee, I don't mean it that way." Jaxson said, straining as he sat upright on the sofa.

"Yeah, you did. And who asked you and where do you get off? You aren't my father and just because you have a chemical engineering degree, that does not mean you are smarter than I am." Her brown eyes flashed so dark they looked black. Lee was furious.

Jaxson was confused and didn't try to hide it. *This woman has gone mad,* he thought. "What? I'm trying not to hurt you! Why are you mad with me?"

"Because who are you to decide what will hurt me? If I pull a man on top of me, I know what it means." She paused. Her eyes focused and she stop pacing. "Why did you leave?" She demanded.

Jaxson's face tightened, but he didn't speak.

"Jaxson, why in the hell did you leave me?"

Eyes fixed on the ground Jaxson refuse to answer.

"And therein lies the problem. You think it's easy to make decisions for others, but not to take ownership of those decisions. I asked you a simple question. And until you can give me an answer, we have nothing else to say to one another."

Lee didn't wait for Jaxson's response. She pivoted angrily and walked out the room.

16

The next morning Jaxson stayed in his room with the door closed. He could hear Jack's small voice inquiring about the closed door and Lee's clipped response. Her voice was low and the words themselves weren't clear, but Lee's tone was unmistakable. For the first time since meeting his brilliant daughter, Jack didn't ask a single follow up question.

He remained silent and still until he heard the angry slam of the door that separated the kitchen from the garage. Earlier, Jaxson had called Natalie and asked her not to come. Jaxson had not slept a wink the night before and he wasn't close to accepting the truth that had been knocking around his chest since Lee had stormed off the night before. He didn't want to explain to Natalie what was wrong with him. Or worse, he didn't want her to guess correctly and give him that look that made him feel like the asshole he was. He needed time to get his shit together and he needed to be alone to do it.

After his last tour of duty and before he'd been relegated to teaching duties, the Marine Corps sent Jaxson to a therapist. He'd volunteer for every assignment and had grown so numbed to the deaths his bombs caused that his superior officer decided he needed to talk to someone. Or else. It helped, but he was still able to easily compartmentalize people and issues to address the problems at hand. That what good Marine's did. What he wasn't good at, apparently, was properly addressing personal, non-war related problems.

He absolutely knew why he'd left Lee. Of course, he did. But to answer her question honestly would only further enflame her anger. Because at the root of it all, she was right. While she was fully capable of taking care of herself, he'd always treated her like he knew better what she could manage. Jaxson had always assumed Lee was fragile. She was quiet and almost always the passive one in their relationship. But what Jaxson had oversimplified in his mind as fear was merely Lee's innate aversion to conflict. The inner strength she had displayed over the last couple of months he'd lived there had truly surprised him. The guilt he'd felt since seeing the real Lee was constant. He'd made a serious miscalculation.

And though he was aware of how his underestimation of Lee had ruined what, by all accounts, was a practically perfect relationship, he'd quickly committed exactly the same stupid act. He was furious with himself. He was sure he'd managed to push Lee away. Again. Just when she'd opened her heart to him. Again.

He had no clue as to what to do. He was so in love with her and he had to find a way to fix things. A simple apology wouldn't work. He'd never seen Lee that angry before. Jaxson concluded that to show Lee he was really different than the kid who'd run, he'd have to reach the levels of brutal honesty that turned his bowels to jelly. But it would be worth it. He realized that Lee and the kids had come to mean everything to him. *I will fix this*, he thought. Jaxson never knew what he wanted out of life beyond his military career, but he now knew he wanted them. Lee was the piece of him that had always been missing.

Decision made, Jaxson called his dad and then his brother, and arranged childcare for Jack and

Dimitri. He knew both kids might be hurt at being shuttled away, especially with the tension between their parents, but this could not wait.

Lee arrived home to find Lukas and Pop waiting for her in the driveway. She hesitated to get out the car but with the kids in the car, her options were to either get out the car or drive away. Lukas must have sensed her hesitation because he quickly moved to stand behind the car, blocking her retreat.

Sighing heavily, she opened the door and stepped out. Pop was standing next to the car door, waiting for her. "Just give him a chance," was all he said as he slid passed her, hopping into the driver's seat. "I'm borrowing my grandkids for dinner and a movie. And I promise to limit their sugar intake," he announced. Lee didn't miss his exaggerated wink that passed through the rearview mirror to Jack nor did she miss Jack's quiet giggle.

He didn't wait for her to agree. He honked twice, fired up the engine, revved it twice then backed out. Jack and Dimitri waved goodbye. She could only stand there and look confused.

Lee started to wonder if she shouldn't question letting him leave with her kids, but before she could say anything Lukas walked out to the street got in his car and drove off. Absently she returned Ava's frantic wave as she watched Lukas' fancy black luxury sedan speed off behind her own car.

Sighing once again, she turned to the house. Lee was fully cognizant that all of this was an effort to get her alone with Jaxson. She should have guessed that this would happen. The fight the night before was the most honest conversation that she and Jaxson had probably ever had.

Lee realized the truth of that sometime during her sleepless night and it gave her a whole new view of their relationship. She was still angry but for all their sakes, she and Jaxson needed to find a happy medium; a way to co-exist and co-parent. Lee didn't regret telling him about Jack or letting him move into their home. But nothing about their relationship was what she'd thought, never had been. And it was proving to be more than she could handle with everything happening with Jaxson and Dimitri. She needed to accept that and move on with her life.

She'd made it to the door when she reached in her jacket pocket and remembered they were in her car. That was gone. With Pop and her children. Opening the storm door to knock, she found the inner door slightly ajar. Lee walked into the nearly silent house and headed straight back to the kitchen. Setting her bag down and shrugging off her suit jacket, she called for Jaxson. He responded that he would be out shortly. Lee went into the refrigerator to grab the bottle of wine she'd put in their earlier that morning. She popped the cork and poured herself a healthy serving in one of her seldom used wine glasses. She sat at the breakfast nook table and sipped, waiting.

Jaxson took a deep breath, grabbed his cane, and hobbled out his room. He'd gone into the kitchen and paused. He'd never seen Lee drink alcohol at dinner, let alone at 4:30 in the afternoon. She lifted her eyes to him as she drained her glass.

"Sit," she ordered as she refilled her glass.

Jaxson considered grabbing a glass for himself, but he figured if she had intended to share the bottle, she would have pulled a glass down for him as well. He sat at the table, folding his hands, and placing them on the table. He leaned forward putting his weight on his elbows. "I know you don't need me," he declared.

Lee froze, stunned, her nearly empty glass halfway to her mouth. Unsure of what to say, she downed the contents and prayed Jaxson didn't need a coherent response. She didn't have one.

But Jaxson quickly continued, "It honestly had never occurred to me that you don't need me. I'm a US Marine Corps officer. I have two chemical engineering degrees. And none of that matters to you. It's all of who I am and none of that matters. Nothing I've accomplished means a damn thing to you. Or Jack. Or Dimitri. Since last night I've been trying to figure out what it is that I bring to the table. You own me, Lee. Heart and soul, body, and mind. You give me balance and sanity. And all I have, and all I am, does nothing for you.

"I didn't know you back then like I thought I did and I sure as hell don't know this wonderful woman and mother you've become. And that's all my fault. I own that. But I do know that Jack is the best parts of me and you... she keeps me moving forward." He'd been staring at his thumbnail, embarrassed and ashamed of this display of his vulnerability. When he finally looked up, Lee had put her wine glass down. Her hands covered her mouth, and tears streamed down her cheeks.

Looking directly into her eyes so there was no questioning his meaning or motive, he said, "I'm so sorry for not seeing that you don't need me to do everything for you, but I want you to know that I need you. I hope to God that I haven't made you not want me anymore." Unable to take her silent tears and unsure of what those tears meant, Jaxson went back to studying the bruised and split thumbnails that protruded from his worn cast.

Lee bolted out of her chair and dropped to her knees grabbing Jaxson's face, "I will always want you. And I do need you. You keep me flexible and not so rigid, which is what flexible means, but you know what I mean. You've brought us joy and carefree happiness, and I didn't realize how much the kids and I needed that." Her tears rolled down her face and fell on his hard boot, and she tried to wipe them away.

Jaxson reached down and pulled Lee's face up to his. He kissed her with everything he felt, everything he had missed and everything he had hoped for. Slowly Jaxson and Lee got to their feet, Jaxson pulling Lee up with him when she held back trying not to put pressure on his leg. They laughed and kissed, melting into each other.

Abruptly Lee pulled away and grabbed Jaxson's hand, pulling him toward his makeshift bedroom. "How long will Lukas and your dad keep the kids tonight," she asked, reaching over to pull Jaxson's shirt off before stripping off her own and slipping out of her bra.

Jaxson froze and his mouth went dry at the sight of her perfectly rounded and delicately peaked brown nipples. Her breasts were better than he'd remembered. Full and heavy, her areoles were a perfect shade of brown that made his mouth water and his cock stiffen. Lost in the thoughts of what he could do with those breasts, he was pulled back to reality by the slacks that flew across the room that landed on his head breaking his stare.

"Jaxson" Lee insisted. His wide eyes flashed up to hers, but his brain wasn't processing rational thought. Lee's eyebrows raised as she waited for some response of the question poses. "The children?" She reminded.

"Later," Jaxson croaked. Lee's nearly nude body played games with his mind. He couldn't breathe. He tried in vain to understand what she was asking, but the thin layer of pink lace that covered the juncture of her long muscular thighs had taken over his mind. Like a zombie, he stumbled forward, fumbling with the strings on his basketball shorts.

Lee put a hand on Jaxson's chest as he pushed forward. She groaned, smacking him on the side of the head, snapping him out of his trance.

"What the hell, Lee" he asked rubbing his earlobe.

She groaned. "Do you want to explain sex to Jack because she walked in on us," Lee asked, one eyebrow cocked in challenge. Jaxson loved that eyebrow so much.

Jaxson blanched. "Oh, God, no." he retorted, wanting to have no part in that interrogation. He tried to remember what he and Lukas had planned. The movie wouldn't start for another 45 minutes.

"We have time." Jaxson relayed the plan to Lee and the mood in the room instantly changed.

He reached out and pulled Lee close. His mouth crushing hers in a searing kiss. Her eyes never leaving his, she untied the knot on his shorts and pulled them down his long firm legs, taking his boxers along with them.

Jaxson pulled back stepping out, his fully erect cock bouncing with desire. "How did you do that without looking," he asked.

Lee laughed, "I'm a mom with two kids. It's one of our inherent superpowers."

"Thank God," Jaxson responded, sliding his hand into Lee's panties. His calloused hands gripped Lee's perfect round backside and gave it a proprietary squeeze, causing moisture to pool between her legs. He took his time kissing down and around her neck and along her collarbone, then between her breasts, stomach and finally the area just above the elastic of her panties, before slowly dragging them down her legs. Somewhat awkwardly, he straightened up and grimaced. Lee smiled and led him to the bed, pushing him down to sit on the edge of the bed. She waited patiently as he gave up control and laid down, giving Lee a sad smile.

"Stop pouting." She chided gently. "You will have plenty of time to ravish me properly in the future. I got this," she moaned bending at the waist and putting Jaxson's happily endowed cock between her lips, sucking gently. Without warning she licked him from tip to base and took nearly the full length of him into her mouth.

Jaxson exhaled slowly and closed his eyes. It had been quite a while since his last sexual encounter with anyone other his hand. Lee's mouth, now rhythmically sliding up and down his shaft, felt better than anything he could remember.

Lee could hear Jaxson's hitched breathing and increased her suction on the head of his cock. He groaned loudly and grabbed her head, pushing himself deeper into her mouth, the head pumping the back of her throat. She fondled his testicles gently as his entire body stiffened.

Unable to handle the sweet torture of Lee's tongue and mouth any longer, Jaxson reluctantly pulled Lee's head away and guided her to straddle him on the bed. Slowly, carefully, but with no shortage of urgency, she lowered herself onto Jaxson's cock, moaning in intense pleasure as his girth stretched her wide. She took several deep breaths waiting for her body to adjust to the intrusion. When the thickness became pleasure, she rode him hard. Hands on his chest but careful not to touch his injuries, feet on the mattress, Lee raised and lowered herself feeling every inch of Jaxson's cock deep in her belly.

Jaxson felt the tightening of his testicles and grabbed Lee's waist hoping to slow her down. Instead, she smiled and increased her speed. She threw her head back and called out his name as her body clenched his cock tightly. Then Jaxson pulled her close, kissing her through her intense orgasm. He wrenched his head to the side as his own gratifyingly powerful orgasm revealed itself. He growled deep and clutched Lee to his chest. She rained light kisses across his neck and chest as they lay there, both out of breath and exhausted. And insanely happy.

17

Lee glanced at the clock and knew she needed to move but lying in Jaxson's arms was too perfect a sensation to disturb. Then, as if on cue, Pop called to make sure it was safe to bring the kids home. Lukas had a sleeping Ava to deal with and had left the movie theater heading straight for home. Jaxson had asked Pop to take the long way home, loathing the fact they both had to go back to their normal life from the bliss they'd found in their lovemaking.

Lee finally pulled herself free from Jaxson's comfortable warmth. She picked up his discarded clothes and left them on his bed, a subtle reminder to re-dress in the same clothes. Then she picked up her clothes and had just made it to the top of the stairs before the doorbell rang.

Lee sprinted into her room and grab her pajamas and robe. Pop must have remembered he had Lee's keys because she could hear the door open followed by the alarms shrill voice announcing the same. She hastily put on her PJs and robe, gathered her hair into a ballerina bun high on her head and hoped against hope that Jack was too tired from her outing for a lengthy interrogation.

No such luck. Jack called for her mom and dad and was running upstairs excited, talking a mile a minute. Lee met her at the top of the stairs and scooped her up "Mommy, grandpa took us for pizza, then we played video games, and he let me drive, then we saw the movie. Dimitri went to sleep on grandpa's lap, but I stayed awake."

"So, you're saying you had fun? Wait – he let you drive? Drive what?" Lee said laughing.

"In the game, mommy," Jack replied. "I'm too little for a car!"

Lee walked down the stairs listening to Jack recall each and every high point from her evening. Pop was seated at the table, looking completely worn out. Lee sat Jack down on the countertop and removed her daughter's jacket and backpack. "Where's Dimitri," Lee asked looking around.

"Same place Jaxson is, knocked out in the den. It was as far as I could carry him. For a three-year-old, that boy is a solid piece of lead." Pop laid his head on the table. "I can't hang! Good thing you guys are young. They have more energy than both of my boys had combined."

Pop groaned loudly, making Jack giggle. He exaggeratedly stood up stretched and said, "I gotta get to bed. Those babies wore me all the way out."

Lee smiled and gave Pop a long tight hug. "It was a long time ago that your boys were this small," Lee said with a smile. "Thanks for everything," she whispered in his ear, then kissed him on the cheek.

"I'm just glad I'm grandpa and don't have to do this every day," Pop laughed and patted Lee's cheek.

"He never did stuff like this when Lukas and I were kids." Jaxson added to Jack with an overly dramatic yawn and caused his father to roll his eyes. "Your grandpa was never this much fun until you guys came along." Jaxson came in holding Dimitri in his good arm and passed him to Lee. "He peed on me," was all he said before turning to Jack. "Madam, did you enjoy yourself?"

Jack smiled big. "Yes. So, are you and mommy getting married now?" Her bright brown eyes swung back and forth between her parents. Pop coughed to cover up his laugh before making a quick retreat from the house. Lee turned toward the stairs to get Dimitri ready for bed. That left Jaxson to answer Jack's questions.

"Really, Lee," Jaxson said through a sigh.

Lee didn't stop walking, only responding, "yep," over her shoulder as she climbed the stairs.

"Daddy," Jack said patiently. "You and mommy made up, right? So... You should get married. That's what grownups do," she stated with far more authority than any four-year-old should be able to muster, even a certified genius.

"Some adults" he started, unsure how to proceed, Jaxson sighed and figured the truth couldn't be any more confusing than the lecture he was conjuring in his head. "Look, you're right. Your mom and I made up, and yes, we are doing better. But sometimes it's better to take things slow and let them fall into place naturally. Does that make sense?"

Jack gave it some thought before nodding. Then she said, "But if you and mommy get married then it would be easier for us to keep Dimitri." She grinned widely, and she clearly knew she was winning – both the battle and the war.

In fact, her eyes were so knowing that it threw Jaxson off a moment. "I'm not sure that's true. Dimitri's grandmother misses her grandson."

"Nah, she's just mean," Jack declared, and dared her dad to challenge her assessment. "Aunt Bryn wouldn't take Dimitri to see her because she's so mean."

Jaxson shook his head. There was no way to soften a conversation to make it palatable to a child when said child was far smarter than you were. He gave up and decided to just tell it like it really was. "You're right. She is and since she thinks I'm dangerous, getting married right now might make things harder for your mom to keep Dimitri."

"But once the judge says Dimitri can stay, you'll get married?" Jack gave her daddy a wide mischievous smile. She had him cornered and she knew it.

Jaxson recognized the exact moment he'd been outsmarted by his daughter. "We'll let that be our little secret." Trying desperately to get out of this conversation before he charted another loss to someone less than five feet tall, he said "time to go to bed."

Jack gave her dad a kiss and a hug before skipping up the stairs, leaving Jaxson to wonder how much of the conversation Lee had overheard.

A month later Lee, Jaxson, Jack, and Dimitri made their way to Lee's family attorney's office. The deposition had been pushed back twice while Jaxson was prepped, and Wilhelmina postured. Lee was a nervous wreck and more than once seriously contemplated packing up the kids and moving to Costa Rica.

Jaxson's lawyer was meeting them there. Jaxson had provided his military records to all parties against Lee's better judgement. He had nothing to hide. Or so he thought.

The questioning was brutal on all fronts. Parts of Jaxson's record and testimony concerned black ops or otherwise classified information, and the JAG officer assigned to him had to work overtime to keep certain information out of the official court record. Wilhelmina's lawyers did their best to paint Jaxson as some crazed government sponsored terrorist. They'd ripped his military psychiatric records to shreds and made him feel like a wild man out to destroy the world. Jaxson's lawyers did their best to rebut their accusations, but their preparations did not take into account the sheer viciousness of Wilhelmina's lawyers.

Wilhelmina arrived at the end of the interview to everyone's shock. She was a frail looking woman, with short, but stylish white hair and angry steel grey eyes. She wore an obviously expensive gray silk suit, sky high heels and carried the most luxurious black handbag Lee had ever seen. The woman oozed money and sophistication. She eyed Dimitri sitting on Jaxson's lap with cold disdain.

"Grandchild," she said with a thick Greek accent. "Come and greet your grandmother properly." She stared intently at Dimitri who burst into tears and tried his best to burrow his entire body into Jaxson's suit jacket. Jack, sensing her brother's distress, ran over to the little boy in full protection mode.

"Stop being mean to Dimitri," Jack yelled before Lee could catch her.

"Jacinta! We don't speak to our elders that way," Lee admonished.

"Poorly raised, just as I would have thought," Wilhelmina scoffed. "You have no business raising my grandson."

Lee fought to control her emotions. She couldn't respond without Jack and Dimitri's hearing it, so she grabbed Jack's arm and plucked Dimitri off Jaxson's lap. She turned toward the door but was stopped by the large man that had accompanied Wilhelmina into the lawyer's conference room. "You may not leave with the Andris heir," he boomed in his heavily accented English.

Jack scrambled back away from the man. She held tight to her mother's leg.

"And you have no right to stop me. I have full custody of Dimitri so get out of my way." Lee said angrily.

The man took a menacing step forward and Lee took an instinctive step back, but her back hit an immovable wall of man behind her. She risked a quick peek over her shoulder and found Jaxson staring a burning hole into the large Greek man's face.

Wilhelmina made a grab for Dimitri, but she was nowhere near as strong as Lee. The older woman fell to the floor as Lee jerked the child away. In all the commotion, Lee managed to scoot out the door with her children in tow. Jaxson opted to stay behind while his and Lee's lawyers argued loudly with Wilhelmina and her legal team. His eyes were trained on the large man that dared to threaten his family.

Jack's reaction to the man hadn't escaped Jaxson's notice. His fist balled up on its own accord, and he was about to knock the bodyguard out when Wilhelmina began to yell.

"This... This is all your fault," came an infuriated voice from the direction of the floor.

Jaxson turned to face her, asking incredulously, "How, exactly, do you figure that?"

"She doesn't need Dimitri," said the old woman. Her accent thickened as she grew angrier, and she was almost unintelligible. "She would have given him to me if you hadn't shown up!"

"Lee loves Dimitri like he's her own. Perhaps if your son hadn't murdered the child's mother, then this wouldn't have happened!" *This woman is truly delusional,* thought a furious Jaxson. "Lee would never willingly give Dimitri to anyone."

"Dom disgraced this family marrying that trash. She drove him to do what he did!" She yelled. "I deserve Dimitri for what that whore did to my son. And once he's mine you and that dark-skinned whore you're shacking up with will never see him again!"

A slight "ahem" sounded from the door. "Mr. Upton, Ms. Anderson is having a hell of a time calming your kids down. Please go down to the lobby and provide her some assistance."

Jaxson turned to the newcomer. A petite black woman with a sharp navy suit and a no-nonsense close-cropped cut for her salt and pepper hair met his gaze and held it.

"Judge Spencer," Dan said rushing over to shake her hand. "Thanks for joining us today." The lawyer pushed Jaxson out the door with a knowing look. Jaxson gave him a terse nod and left them in the conference room following the maze of hallways and doors that led to the lobby from the office.

After having to double back twice, he finally exited the office suite Jaxson heard Dimitri's terrified screams and Jack's muffled sobs. "Dimitri", he said in the same tone he used with his soldiers. The child looked up and leapt off Lee's lap. Running as fast as his little legs could carry him, Dimitri made it to his dad and leapt into his arms.

Jaxson held onto the boy, who repeated the word 'no' between sobs. Dimitri so rarely spoke that it took Jaxson a moment to decipher it.

"No one is going to take you from your mama," he said, trying his hardest to reassure the wailing child. "But if you don't calm down, you'll make yourself throw up all over our new suits and mommy is going to be really unhappy!"

Dimitri's eyes went wide, and he fought his sobs and tried to calm down, but he was in the midst of a complete tantrum. Jaxson carried the boy outside and let him finish crying at full volume. Just as Dimitri calmed down and was falling asleep, Lee and Jack came out of the building.

"Dan's assistant said we can go home. We are done apparently." Lee said, clearly confused. "I know the mediator had arrived, and I figured I needed to be there, but Suzette said no." Lee thought about it for a moment then shrugged her shoulders. She was too tired and upset to fight with anyone else at the moment.

"Uh... that wasn't a mediator. That was your judge showing up and she saw firsthand the real Wilhelmina," Jaxson said shyly.

Lee's eyes went wide. "That sweet woman that stopped to help me - was the judge?" Lee's face went pale and she began to sniffle and tear up.

Confused, Jaxson asked "Honey, what's wrong?"

Lee responded by rushing to the car, Jack still in her arms. She couldn't maneuver the keys and the sleeping child, so she lost it. Lee burst into frustrated tears, crying almost uncontrollably. She looked for Jaxson through the silent tears as he caught up to her and he laid a hand on her shoulder to offer some support. "Talk to me," he said.

She shook her head. "Help me get the kids in the car first."

So, they did. Jack first, then Dimitri. Lee got in the driver's seat and started the car, cracking the windows in the front so the two could nap safely and in peace. Lee looked at her babies in the rearview mirror and nearly fell apart again. A knock on the window brought Lee out of her thoughts.

She stepped out of the sedan to face Jaxson.

"Fuck, Jaxson! The judge saw me struggling with the kids. Dimitri was terrified, and Jack was so confused she went into a temper tantrum too. Then Jack wanted me to pick her up, but I was already carrying Dimitri and the whole thing was terrible. The judge is never going to let me keep Dimitri. I know she thinks I can't handle being a parent."

Jaxson peeked at the kids to make sure they were still asleep. Especially Jack. Satisfied they hadn't heard what she'd said and was not about to be questioned to within an inch of his life, Jaxson turn to Lee.

He pulled her into his arms and smiled. Lee tried to pull away, but Jaxson held her tight and said, "Let me explain."

Lee relaxed her body and gave Jaxson the benefit of the doubt.

"After you and the babies left, Wilhelmina lost her shit. The judge heard every foul thing Wilhelmina said about you. And me and the kids too. Wilhelmina is an angry crazy old woman."

She stood there, completely stunned hearing that the judge knew how much Wilhelmina didn't like her, and not just because she was black. Lee didn't know what to say.

Jaxson further explained, "I think you could do anything short of beating them in public with a police baton and still keep custody of the kids."

Lee squealed and jumped into Jaxson's arms kissing him soundly.

"God, mommy, what's happening?" Came a grumpy voice from the backseat of the car.

Jaxson and Lee laughed. "Sorry honey," Lee whispered softly. "I'll try to keep it down."

Jaxson turned Lee's face up to his and kissed her soundly on the lips. "Let's go home, Jaxson said.

"Better idea - let's go get some ice cream" Lee suggested. That got Jack's attention. She hooted loudly and woke up her brother. He was still sleepy and therefore less enthusiastic about the prospect of having ice cream before dinner than his sister. The little boy had gone back to sleep before they'd driven out of the parking lot.

19

Dimitri simply would not stop fidgeting. Jaxson had promised to take him to the park to drive the new remote-control car he had gotten for his fourth birthday if he was a good boy while they were in court. However, he had become extremely impatient waiting for the adoption ceremony to start.

"Mommy is the judge coming," Dimitri asked for the fourth time in twenty minutes.

Jack rolled her eyes. A mature five-year-old now, she had no patience for her brother's childish antics. "You need to calm down, Dimitri. Judges have to take their time because they make important decisions. I'm gonna be a judge just like Judge Spencer," Jack announced for what had to be the fortieth time that week.

Dimitri reared back to respond, but his mother's sharp look caused him to bite back his remark. In the last few months Dimitri had really come out of his shell. He now talked non-stop trying to keep up with his sister's inquisitive nature. He had even started to become a little social butterfly at daycare. Lee felt confident Jaxson's solid influence was the reason they'd all become so much happier.

She turned to Jaxson and smiled. She was happy, really happy that she had given their relationship another chance. And when he'd proposed a few weeks ago, she was thrilled to say, "Yes".

And of course, Jack had at least two dozen questions. The last of which was when was her mom going to have another baby. Lee just brushed the question off, but she knew the answer. Jack and Dimitri were going to have a brother or sister in about six months. She'd finally gotten the confirmation call from her doctor.

The judge came out of her chambers and took her bench, smiling widely at the new little family.

"Our first order of business is to finalize the adoption of Dimitri Bryant Andris by Lee Kamila Anderson." The Bailiff brought the papers forward for Lee to sign. Dimitri's brilliant smile went from ear to ear.

Lee turned to Dimitri and hugged him tightly. "Now you are stuck with me forever, kiddo." She kissed him loudly on the cheek and, to her surprise he wiggled, but didn't wipe it off as he had started doing recently.

She wiped the lipstick off his cheek with her thumb and stood up to find the judge standing behind of her.

Smiling at the confused look on Lee's face, the judge said, "and on to the second order of business."

The door opened at the back of the courtroom. Lukas was first carrying a prettily dressed Ava in his arms. Pop followed, carrying flowers and a large white bag. And behind them were Lee's mother and sister.

Lee was dumbfounded. "How? What?" She stumbled over her word trying to formulate a sentence, but she was unable to get her thoughts together.

Lee's mother and sister had gone back to Kenya to live after her father had died. After Jaxson was injured and had moved in with them, she'd canceled the trip she'd had planned for her and the kids to visit them. Her mom's declining health had made overseas travel impossible, or so Lee had thought.

Dimitri scurried to Pop and took the flowers he held. Turning back to his mom, who was now crying, he held them out to her.

"These are yours, mama." He declared. When she didn't respond, he said "Mom! Girls hold flowers when they get married, right? Daddy said I could walk you down the aisle because your daddy died."

Lee's quiet sobs turned into a loud blubber. Jaxson stepped forward, leading Lee's mom. He released the older woman's arm and pulled Lee into a tight hug.

"I sincerely hope those are tears of joy," he said laughing.

Lee buried her face into his neck, and tried to nod a "yes" around her hiccups. Then, as though she just realized it, she pulled away and grabbed her mother and pulled her close.

"Lee Kamila, stop all this blubbering!" Her mother demanded. "You are holding up your own wedding." The sound of her mother's warm voice and the woman's perfect English paired with the tinge of an accent sent Lee into another round of tears. She turned to Lee's sister and said, "Lucy say something or Lee's tears will soak through my sweater."

Lucy laughed. "I've never seen her act like this. Maybe she's having a breakdown."

Lee let her mom go and tried to calm her breathing. "Shut up brat," she said before embracing her beloved yet endlessly annoying younger sister.

"Hi Grandma, hi Aunt Lucy" Jack said getting everyone's attention. Jack waved though she held her dad's hand tightly.

"Wait! You've met each other?" Lee was truly confused. She fixed her gaze on Jaxson and waited for his explanation.

"The judge agreed to marry us," was all he was able to say while she stared so intently at him.

"Jaxson!" Lee warned.

He laughed and explained the rest. "When you accepted my proposal, I reached out to your mom and sister not knowing what needed to happen or how long it would take to bring them back to Charlotte. Then Dimitri's final adoption date was set and I started working on this surprise. I know how much you've missed them. Jack went with me to the airport to pick up Eunice and Lucy. So, yes, they've met."

"Grandma said I can visit her in Kenya if you say it's okay," Jack added quickly.

Lee's eyes threatened to run over with tears again. "Of course, it's okay," she whispered.

"Lee, in all the years I've known you, I may have seen you cry twice. Lately you've been nothing but a mess of tears. Are you ok?" Jaxson frowned and placed a hand on her forehead to check for a fever.

Lee smiled then laughed. "That's because you were on deployment the last time I was pregnant. You missed all the tears!"

Jaxson's face blanched, but everyone else laughed and offered congratulations.

"Good thing you two are getting married then," the judge remarked with a smile.

Quickly, everyone took their places. Lee held Dimitri's hand and Jack stood as her daddy's best girl, with Lukas next to her holding the rings. Pop, Ava, Eunice, and Lucy sat together on the first row of seats in the courtroom.

As she reached Jaxson's side, Lee bent down and kissed Dimitri and sent him to sit next to Lucy. Then she turned forward, taking Jaxson's hand. His face was still ashen from the news.

"You're not the only one who can plan a surprise," she whispered and laughed. Her life couldn't be any better.

ABOUT THE AUTHOR

Lori A Hendricks is an IT project manager by day and science fiction/fantasy novelist by night. A longtime lover of words, she reads science fiction, fantasy, and paranormal romance novels regularly (when there is time). When not reading, writing, or working, Lori can most often be found watching football or basketball and yelling insanely at the television.

Also by Lori A Hendricks:

Fairytale Lost
Half Breed Queen
Amethyst Rising
Skatia Reborn